Laying Claim

A Rough Edges Series Book 1

by

Matthew Dante

Laying Claim

Copyright ©2022 Matthew Dante

All rights reserved.

Cover by **The Ravens Touch** @the.ravens.touch

Proofread by Black Quill Editing

No part of this publication may be reproduced, stored in a retrieval system, or transmitted in any form or by any means—electronic, mechanical, photocopying, and recording, or otherwise—without prior written permission from the author. The exception would be brief passages by a reviewer in a newspaper or magazine or online. To perform any of the above is an infringement of copyright law.

This book is a work of fiction. Names, characters, places, and incidents either are products of the author's imagination or are used fictitiously. Any resemblance to actual persons, living or dead, events, or locales is entirely coincidental.

Warning: This book contains scenes that may be considered triggering events for some involving violence, murder, and drug and alcohol use.

ISBN: 978-1-7779446-2-9

CONTENTS

Prologue- Mickey 1

CHAPTER 1- Mickey 8

CHAPTER 2- Seth 15

CHAPTER 3- Mickey 23

CHAPTER 4- Seth 39

CHAPTER 5- Mickey 44

CHAPTER 6- Mickey 53

CHAPTER 7- Seth 67

CHAPTER 8- Seth 79

CHAPTER 9- Mickey 83

CHAPTER 10- Seth 98

CHAPTER 11- Mickey 109

CHAPTER 12- Seth 113

CHAPTER 13- Seth 123

CHAPTER 14- Mickey 134

CHAPTER 15- Seth 143

CHAPTER 16- Seth	156
CHAPTER 17- Seth	171
CHAPTER 18- Mickey	184
CHAPTER 19- Seth	196
CHAPTER 20- Mickey	202
CHAPTER 21- Seth	215
CHAPTER 22-Seth	225
CHAPTER 23- Mickey	240
CHAPTER 24- Seth	248
CHAPTER 25- Mickey	261
CHAPTER 26-Seth	271
CHAPTER 27- Mickey	279
CHAPTER 28- Seth	285
Epilogue- Mickey	290
ABOUT THE AUTHOR	299
ACKNOWLEDGEMENT	300
OTHER BOOKS BY MATTHEW DANTE	301

Prologue- Mickey

"It's my turn!" the young boy yelled, smashing his fist against the *Sorry!* game board. Several of the blue and red pegs went flying out of their holes, scattering across the carpeted floor.

"No, it's not. You just went, then you went pee, now it's my turn, Toby." Calm green eyes looked up at his friend as he began replacing the pieces that had been disturbed. "You always forget, and then get mad."

Toby crossed his arms against his chest and huffed. The boy was one year younger than Mickey and struggled with a short temper. Mickey was used to these outbursts and didn't mind. He liked playing with Toby. When he was with Toby, it felt like having a little brother. Momma always said that older brothers had to have patience and always look out for their little brothers. While Toby was not actually Mickey's younger brother, he liked to pretend he was. He didn't feel so . . . lonely.

Momma had explained that God had only blessed them with one child and that his Momma was not able to give him a younger brother or sister. But not to worry, because the world was filled with lots of other boys and girls who were looking for other siblings as well. Other kids they could play with and protect one another.

When Mickey met Toby, he realized that Toby could be his younger brother. They could play together, read comics together, and he would even look after Toby like a big brother should.

Once all the pieces were back in their place, Mickey pushed the board toward Toby. "Here, you can take your turn."

Toby's face lit up with the news that it was his turn to play. He pressed down on the plastic dome and impatiently waited until the dice stopped moving.

Deep down, Mickey knew it was not Toby's turn, but seeing his friend's face light up the way it did, told him he had done something good.

When it was Mickey's turn, he pressed down on the dome and held it firmly in place. He imagined he was charging up his superpowers, getting ready to supercharge the dice. He counted to three, then let go, watching the dice as they flipped with lightning speed.

"Yes!" Mickey cheered when the dice landed on six. He only needed to move six more spaces to win the game.

Realizing his friend would be disappointed by his pending victory, Mickey decided to use some 'creative' counting. He moved the pieces, counting slowly, being sure to accidentally move two spots on one count, thereby ensuring he did not win.

"Yes!" Toby cheered, pumping his fist up and down. "You lose!"

Mickey chuckled. While he hadn't exactly lost the game yet, he was glad his best friend was still happy. "Shit. Not fair. I was so close."

Both boys jumped as they heard the sound of a trash can falling over outside. They both looked at each other, frightened.

Mickey's father had told both boys to stay in his office and play while he went outside to talk to the other grownups.

Toby's eyes were wide as he stared at Mickey. "What was that?"

"Probably just a stray cat knocking somethin' over." Mickey looked over his shoulder toward the door, knowing very well it was most likely not a cat.

There was something about the way his father had insisted they remain inside to play and not come out that had Mickey worried. What if his father was hurt? What if he'd fallen down and couldn't get back up?

The old man, two houses down had fallen in his shower and bumped his head. Then he died because no one came to help him. What if his Pops had fallen and needed help, too? Perhaps he should go take a quick peek. Just to make sure.

"Where are you going?" Toby asked, as Mickey opened the office door and poked his head out.

No one was around.

"Stay here. I'm just going to check if Pops is all right."

"What about my dad? I want to check on him too. What if they both fell down?" Toby's voice sounded much younger than six.

"Fine. Come with me, you little shit, but make sure no one sees you, or Pops will tan my hide."

Cool air rushed in as Mickey slowly pushed the backdoor of the bar open. He could hear his father shouting something and what sounded like grunts and moans.

Mickey was scared and wanted to run back into the office and hide, but he kept going. He needed to be a brave boy. What if his father was hurt and needed his help? Maybe Pops was in trouble.

Mickey's breath caught in his chest as he felt Toby's shaking hand slide into his. He squeezed his palm, hoping to provide some sort of comfort to his best friend. He needed to be brave . . . for the both of them.

The voices got louder as the boys approached the back of the building. Slowly, the boys peeked around the corner, then gasped.

Toby's father lay on his back coughing up blood while Mickey's father straddled him, punching the man in the face repeatedly.

"No fuckin' homo is gonna work for my crew!" Clive growled between punches. His Irish accent was thick with fury. "Marie saw ye kissing that dude last night behind the bar. You think I want some pansy-ass, cocksucker hanging out with me and my crew?"

"Clive, please. It's not like that," Sean pleaded through a mouthful of blood.

The sound of Toby's father sobbing and scared frightened Mickey. Why was his father hurting Toby's dad? Why was Toby's dad crying? Mickey was so confused and scared. He didn't know what was happening or what to do.

"Dad!" Toby shouted from behind Mickey as he darted out from their hiding spot running toward his father's battered body.

"Toby!" Mickey shouted, but it was too late. His best friend already had his arms wrapped around his father, crying.

"What the . . . ?" Clive uttered, taking a step back from the crying boy gripping his father.

Mickey could feel the tears begin to form as he watched his friend clinging to his beaten dad. Why had Pops done this? Why had he hurt Toby's dad? They were friends . . . weren't they?

"You're supposed to be inside!" Clive yelled at Mickey, making him jump.

Clive waved to the other men currently standing in a semi-circle watching the beating take place. The men moved in and pulled Toby from his father, before proceeding to help Sean to his feet.

Clive walked over to where Mickey stood shaking with fear. He knelt down so his face was level with his son's.

"This is what happens to homos. They get their ass beat. You best make sure you stay the fuck away from those perverted queers. And if I ever catch ye making out with one of them, I'll beat yer scrawny arse till you're black and blue. Is that clear?"

Mickey nodded his head, terrified of his father. There was no way he was ever going to kiss a boy and get beaten by his father as Sean had. The thought terrified him.

Clive pulled his son close to his body as he walked with him back into the bar. Mickey watched as a drop of blood fell from his father's hand to his shoulder, staining his transformers T-shirt. Was that blood from Toby's dad?

Mickey glanced over his shoulder at his friend, who had his face buried in his father's chest, sobbing. It was in that moment that Mickey realized his friend would never forgive him for what Clive had done.

Their friendship had come to an end.

Mickey's father was poison and would end up being the cause of so much pain for Mickey in the coming years. Mickey had yet to discover this for himself.

With a quiet tear, he silently said goodbye to his best

friend and adoptive little brother. Deep down, Mickey knew this was the last time he would ever see Toby.

CHAPTER 1 - Mickey

The yellow and black Caution Tape reflected off the large puddle, warning people of the horrific scene they were about to encounter. The alleyway was dark and smelled of rotten food, garbage, and urine—typical smells found in any downtown Jersey alleyway.

The rain had mostly stopped, but the surfaces remained sleek and slippery. Perhaps it was a blessing that it had rained earlier, as the excess water was slowly carrying away the blood that currently trickled from the dead man's head. A steady stream of crimson water flowed down to the street, carrying away evidence of the spine-chilling death that had occurred just hours ago.

The moon was still high, and it would be hours before people would begin their morning routines.

In the alleyway, lay the mangled body of a young man, covered in tattoos, who had apparently decided to take a swan dive off the roof of the adjacent building. The body lay sprawled across the pavement, head facing in the opposite direction than God intended. The man's eyes stood open, caught in the vacant stare of some unknown image.

At first glance, one would assume the body was a prop used while making some sort of slasher film, but sadly, this was not a horror movie and most certainly not a fake corpse.

This was the type of crime scene that gave first responders nightmares for years to come.

The victim was only twenty-one years old. Barely a man these days. Well, that's not entirely true. On the streets of Jersey, you become a man at the age of thirteen. You learn to fight at fifteen and get your first taste of pussy when you are sixteen. By seventeen, most guys have been in juvie at least once and by nineteen, several are either dealing, running guns, or working deliveries for the O'Brien crime family.

The streets of Jersey City were a rough and mean place to live. The area was run and protected by the O'Brien crime family, a criminal enterprise with roots leading back to Ireland.

Clive O'Brien was the current head of the family and had been overseeing operations for the past fifteen years; ever since Clive Sr. decided to piss off the wrong Italian gangster in New York. They eventually found Clive Sr.'s body encased in concrete.

A valuable lesson was learned that day, don't piss off an Italian mobster. Especially one who owned a construction company.

Clive Jr. didn't seem all that sad when his father went missing and he had to step into his role as leader.

"Poor kid," a voice whispered from beside Mickey.

Mickey turned his head slightly. His best friend emerged from the darkness.

Patrick's eyes were focused on the lifeless body of the boy they used to call "Beep." The boy's real name was Jasper, but he was given the nickname Beep due to his aversion to swearing—imitating a beeping sound whenever he accidentally swore.

Beep's fear of swearing stemmed back to his mother's constant threats of "Smacking his face so hard, that his head would spin."

His momma was a foul-tempered Irish woman, who would no doubt have kept her promise of extreme violence if she ever caught her son cursing.

Looking back on her words, there was almost a tragic foreboding to her constant threats of violence.

"No one should ever have to die that way," Mickey said, turning his attention back to Beep.

The positioning of his body was so unnatural. His neck had done a complete one-eighty; his left arm was broken and rested bent behind his back and his right leg stretched unnaturally to the right.

"The poor kid must have bounced off those fire escapes

as he fell to the ground." Mickey turned to look at Patrick. "How else would his body have landed like that?"

Patrick's brilliant green eyes looked especially fierce tonight as they reflected the light from the moon. "Beep makes three."

Mickey closed his eyes as his jaw tightened. He hoped it was just a coincidence, but now it was starting to look more and more like a pattern. A pattern that pointed directly at the O'Brien crew.

Two other crew members had died horrible deaths over the past few months. One of his dealers had run out in front of a truck while shouting nonsense. Then last month, one of his drivers had taken a gun to his head in a fit of rage and panic. Those with him at the time thought he had taken some bad acid or something, chalking it up to an unfortunate accident.

But seeing Beep's mangled body on the asphalt after taking a dive off the side of a building . . . all these tragic accidents were starting to look less and less like accidents at all.

"Do you really think someone is targeting the crew?"

Patrick's face hardened. "I hate to say it, but there have been way too many freak accidents lately, brother. I think it might be worth takin' a look into."

While Mickey was the older of the two—by two years—he trusted Patrick's opinion without question. The two were basically brothers. They had been best friends since Mickey was ten, and Patrick was eight.

Being the older of the two, Mickey leaned into the role of big brother, never letting anyone mess with Patrick. That was until Patrick turned fifteen and became a massive wall of muscle that didn't need protecting. Since then, the two had been looking out for one another.

That was how you earned trust on the streets of Jersey. It was earned over time and based on one's unwavering loyalty.

"Fine. See what you can find out. But keep it quiet. I don't want the rest of the crew getting nervous. Nervous Irish men who love their whiskey are never a healthy combo."

"What about your old man?"

"I'll let the old bastard know later today. I wish he would just hurry up and die already. Tired of his fucked-up mentality and ancient ways." Mickey was the one and only son of Clive O'Brien, head of the New Jersey crime family.

Mickey was next in line to take over the family business once his father finally kicked the bucket or stepped aside—which was highly unlikely. Powerful men like Clive tend not to let go of their reign of terror voluntarily.

"Best of luck with that one. Can I have your car when you're done?" Patrick joked, knowing Clive's temper was legendary.

"You're a real arse sometimes, you know that, you dumb shite." Mickey shook his head trying not to crack a smile. They were standing in front of one of their dead friends after all.

"So, which one of you assholes wants to come down to the station and answer a few questions? I assume this ballerina here belongs to you?" A balding, pudgy officer stepped under the police tape and made his way over to where Mickey and Patrick were standing.

"Evening, Officer Shear," Mickey greeted as the officer approached.

Mickey's crew was intimately familiar with most of the Jersey City Police having either been arrested by them or having gone to school with most of them. There were few options for young Irish kids in Jersey, most chose one of the three easy Cs: construction, crew life, or cop.

Officer Shear was one such kid. He had gone to school with Mickey and had even spent Saturdays playing rugby with Mickey and some of the other crew members he regularly arrested while growing up.

"His name was Jasper Murphy. I'll come with you down to the station." Mickey nodded toward the uniformed officer.

Jasper had mostly worked behind the scenes for Mickey and had only recently started working on the streets as one of his drug dealers. He had managed to remain off Officer Shear's radar, up until now that was.

"Can we stop and grab a bagel and some coffee on the way?" Mickey placed his arm around the officer's shoulders as he walked with him back to his cruiser.

After a few steps, Mickey stopped and turned back to his friend. "Hey, Paddy!" He watched as Patrick looked up from his phone. "Get one of the guys to take my car back to my condo." He tossed his keys to Patrick, who caught them with his left hand and grimaced.

Patrick knew that "one of the boys" meant him. Mickey trusted no one with his baby but Patrick. Mickey smirked, knowing how much Patrick hated being his errand boy.

Satisfied his beloved vehicle was in capable hands, Mickey slapped Officer Shear's shoulder, leading him away from the crime scene and off to grab breakfast before heading to the station.

CHAPTER 2 - Seth

Music from Ashanta's latest hit single blared throughout the warehouse. Every few feet, women danced on risers in the tiniest bikinis that threatened to snap with even the slightest hint of a breeze.

Complimenting these dancing beauties, were mouthwatering men who wore nothing more than a strategically placed golden leaf, some leaves being much larger than others. These men laid on golden pillars that kept rising and lowering to the beat of the music.

From the far side of the room, Seth watched in awe as Eve, one of his best friends, seductively danced around Ashanta as she belted out the chorus to one of her biggest songs this summer, *Play Dirty*.

Seth still couldn't believe Eve had scored a part in Ashanta's music video. He also, couldn't believe he was currently standing on set, watching one of his favorite singers dance with one of his best friends. He felt like he was standing in a dream.

The set was closed to the general public, but Eve had arranged for Seth to be granted special access so he could meet his favorite singer.

As Seth watched the sexy dancers and flashing lights, he couldn't help but feel his gay fierceness struggling to set herself free.

Slowly his legs began to twitch, then his hips began to roll. Next thing he knew his shoulders were flying back as his gay fierceness took control.

The gay force was strong with this one. He didn't care what people thought. Ashanta's music spoke to people and right now his body was saying "Shake that ass like you're competing against a room full of bottoms!" And judging by some of the muscle queens dancing on the columns, he might have his work cut out for him.

The music video was a sea of gorgeous men and women dancing all around Ashanta—their queen. Whoever had dreamed up the concept for this video should be commended. It was hot as fuck. Seth wanted nothing more than to dance and grind with the entire cast currently thrusting their pelvises into the air.

What he wouldn't give to have one of those men hold him down and plow into him. Fuck. He needed to get laid.

Seth was jerked from his happy thoughts when the music came to a sudden halt.

The dancers looked relieved that they finally got a break, while the tantalizing men quickly rushed to cover their junk that was currently on full display.

"That's a wrap for today!" the director, a new up-and-coming gay queen from Spain, called out to everyone.

Seth watched as Eve put her arm around Ashanta and pointed at Seth. He could feel his palms sweat and suddenly he was forgetting how to breathe . . .

Was it one in and two out? Or two out and one in? What? Why was this so difficult?

Calm the fuck down. She's only a woman—a woman who has the voice of an angel and the dance moves of a goddess. No Biggy. She's just coming over to say hi and see what a complete spaz you are.

Seth quickly rubbed his hands against his jeans, hoping to remove any dampness. He was about to meet a goddess and the last thing he needed was sweaty hands.

"Ashanta, this is my 'gay in training' and sweet friend, Seth. He has the biggest hardon for you. But don't worry, this little twinkie plays for my team, and has a bad case of sausage addiction. So, you don't have to worry about him trying to sleep with you. Your boobies are his kryptonite." Eve winked at Seth, giving him a teasing smile.

Ashanta burst out laughing and leaned in to hug Seth. "Wow! It's so nice to meet you, Seth. Eve was right. You are a delicious little treat."

Now it was Seth's turn to blush and die of embarrassment. Was he really being complemented by his queen? His idol? "It's so nice to meet you as well. I can't believe I'm actually hugging you. I'm totally fangirling right now. I'm a huge fan in case you haven't guessed."

Seth was still in shock and trying to remain in his body. "I have to say, you have the voice of an angel."

Ashanta's face lit up. "Oh my god, I love you. You're right, Eve, he is just the sweetest man."

"I told you he was. This diva has been teaching her little twinkie how to behave himself." Eve reached over and hugged Seth from the side.

The three spoke for a few minutes until Ashanta was dragged away by the director to discuss tomorrow's shots.

"Give me fifteen minutes to quickly change, then we can get out of here." Eve held down her tits as she ran off behind a partition, presumably to change out of the dental floss outfit and into more appropriate New York street attire.

Eve had transitioned from Evan to Eve a few years back, and Seth couldn't help but admire Eve's smoking hot body. Seth was as gay as they came, but he could still appreciate the look of a sexy woman's body.

Silently, he watched as several of the hunky pillar dancing men threw their bags over their shoulders, laughing and chatting as they left the building. Secretly, he longed to be one of those guys. Someone who was idolized and drooled over whenever he walked into a room.

Not to say that Seth wasn't attractive. Lots of men propositioned him all the time. He was young, fit, and smart. The so-called gay trifecta.

He figured it was one of the gay genes that caused a

lack of self-confidence in every gay man. A need to be wanted, desired, and seen by all men.

At that moment, his thoughts drifted to Ivan—Marc and Alex's mysterious friend, who he had met last fall. When Seth met Ivan, they had spent hours laughing and chatting over wine in Alex's living room. Ivan made it pretty clear that he was interested in Seth, even asking for his number so they could grab a drink together.

But of course, nothing had materialized. Ivan suddenly disappeared and Seth was left wondering how it was possible that he had driven away yet another potential suitor.

Guys were ridiculous. Was no one interested in a serious relationships anymore? Was he doomed to be alone forever?

Once Eve finished changing, they walked down the street and grabbed coffees from one of the street vendors. It was a nice day out, so they absentmindedly strolled behind a mother and her four-year-old daughter, following them into one of the dozens of parks scattered across the city.

In the center of the park was a large water fountain that seemed to be home to a flock of pigeons. Seth took a seat on the ledge, enjoying the view and sipping his coffee.

"So, how are the plans coming along?" Eve asked, giving cut-eye to one of the pigeons who was taking baby steps toward them.

"What plans?" Seth asked, knowing full well which

plans Eve was referring to.

"I don't know . . . plans for a night of debauchery and sin. One last celebration of freedom before being locked away by the powers of marriage and commitment." Eve threw her arms in the air as she mimicked breaking her chains above her head.

The woman had a flair for the dramatic. It was one of the things people loved about her. She had such an energetic and powerful personality.

"Like you aren't already disgustingly committed to one another. I swear you two share one shadow." Seth smirked at the thought.

Eve dropped her arms and directed her cut-eye at Seth. "Yeah, I guess there is something about the gigantic nerd that has me under his spell. I still want to have one night of naked men dancing around with their cocks flopping about." Eve shook her head back and forth, imitating being beaten in the face by several dicks at once.

Seth chuckled. "Don't worry, there will be lots of naked men and sweaty balls all up in your face."

"Don't tease a girl with a good time."

Seth admired Eve. She had met her fiancé, James, a few years ago while they were in university. The two were complete opposites; Eve was loud and adventurous, while James was shy and reserved. Yet, the two fit together perfectly.

While Eve joked about naked men and being cock

slapped in her face, Seth knew deep down, Eve would never cheat on James or do anything that would hurt his feelings.

Eve hated to admit it, but she was madly in love with the gigantic nerd.

Seth hoped that one day he too would be able to find such a loving and committed relationship. Perhaps there was a guy out there who would see him for who he really was. The man behind the mask he showed the world.

Deep down, the only thing Seth really wanted was to be loved. To have someone he could trust and rely on. Someone who would be there for him, protect him, and make him smile when he was feeling down. Someone who would believe him when he asked for help . . .

Seth's gaze drifted off as he thought about his parents. A dark shadow fell over his face as his mind was invaded by the hurtful memories of his past.

"Hey, love. Is everything okay?" Eve's voice cut through the darkness, bringing Seth's mind back into focus.

"Hmm?" Seth murmured, emerging from the fog in his mind.

"You kind of went all emo there for a sec. Is everything okay?"

Seth took a deep breath, shaking away the painful memories. "Yeah, everything's fine. Just thought about my folks there for a sec."

Eve's expression softened. "Still no word from them?"

"No, and I don't expect there to be. They're the ones who betrayed me. They are the ones who have to make amends with me. I'm better off without them anyway." Seth felt defeated. "You guys are my family now." He leaned his head against Eve's shoulder. He wanted to be comforted, but he also wanted to hide the true expression on his face.

Eve and the rest of the gang assumed Seth no longer spoke to his parents because they did not accept his sexuality. But truth be told, Seth was far too embarrassed to tell them the real reason he'd left home and no longer spoke to his parents. The feeling of hurt and betrayal was just too much for Seth to handle.

Eve wrapped her arm around Seth's shoulders and kissed the top of his head. "Trust me, love, those assholes don't deserve to have such a sweety in their lives. We are all the family you will ever need."

Eve's words warmed Seth's heart. While they may not be related by blood, Eve, James, Marc, and Alex were his chosen family. They welcomed him into their little group of gay misfits with open arms.

But still, he hoped to find that special someone. That one guy, who belonged just to him.

Someday . . .

CHAPTER 3 - Mickey

Ye' Old Pint was an old Irish pub that had operated in the neighborhood for over sixty years. Originally, the pub was owned by a lovely elderly Irish couple who opened the bar when they first came to America back in the 1960s.

Back then the locals were not the most welcoming or trusting of those of Irish descent and it was not uncommon for those with green in their blood to suffer unwarranted abuse or harassment.

As the years passed, the tight-knit Irish community worked together to take care of each other and provide support where needed.

One family, above all, took it upon themselves to ensure that the Irish people and their community were protected. The O'Briens.

In the 1960s, the O'Brien family consisted of three brothers who preferred to make a living off the seedier underbelly of society. Starting with gambling and prostitution, the brothers quickly ventured into drugs and weapons sales, recruiting nearly three-quarters of the Irish male population in their community to work for their quickly expanding organization.

The O'Briens looked out for their community and made sure their people were protected and treated fairly.

Local establishments appreciated having people they knew and trusted looking out for them and often did what they could to help contribute to the empire being built by the O'Briens. Sometimes they offered the use of one of their trucks, other times they offered the use of one of their storage rooms to store 'product' for the O'Briens.

When all was said and done, the Irish in Jersey looked out for one another and stuck together.

Over the years, ownership of Ye' Old Pint passed through multiple individuals. When the Shaws retired, they passed the pub to their son, who then lost it gambling to a friend, who eventually sold it to Clive O'Brien, who then gifted the bar to his son, Mickey, on his twenty-first birthday. Not a bad gift for someone just turning twenty-one.

The pub had been owned by many people, but through it all, the place remained the same; a safe place for the local Irish community to come, relax, and enjoy a pint with their friends.

Mickey patted Cillian, one of their newest servers, on the back as he entered the bar. "Hey, Cillian. How's it going?"

"A' right. Not a bad one so far, yeah!" Cillian hollered over his shoulder as he cleared the empty beer bottles and glasses from a vacated booth. "Should pick up a bit mo' as the night progresses."

Cillian—pronounced *kill-ee-an* for those not accustomed to the Irish tongue—was new to the States, so his Irish accent came out rather thick. He liked to joke that his accent was his superpower. Once he opened his mouth to speak, women's panties flew off. Judging by all the pussy the man seemed to get, Mickey was pretty sure Cillian was right.

At twenty-seven, Cillian had the fit body of a man with the sexual appetite of a nineteen-year-old. He kept the bar filled with young ladies who were always looking for a good time, so Mickey didn't give a shit where Cillian was sticking his dick.

Mickey tapped his fist on the bar and nodded to Gale, who was busy pouring a pint for one of their customers. She gave a slight nod as she tilted the glass upward. Only in a bar was getting too much head a bad thing.

Gale was one tough-looking woman. She was in her late thirties, had tattoos running down both her arms, and had recently gotten a nose ring. Her hair was badass: The left side of her head was shaved short with the top longer, parted, and hanging over the right side of her face.

It was a total balance of masculinity and femininity that gave Gale a don't-fuck-with-me vibe. She fucked big, burly bikers nightly and sucked titties with rocker chicks when the mood struck. Mickey loved her style.

As he made his way through the bar, Mickey slapped the backs of a few of their regulars, who enjoyed late afternoon drinking. Some of these guys were unemployed and often did a few odd jobs for Mickey and his crew as a way to earn some extra cash . . . others were here trying to hide from their wives.

Mickey didn't judge. All these guys were like family. They were his people, and he had a responsibility to look after them.

Once he passed through the door at the back of the bar, he walked through the small kitchen where Sal was preparing a batch of wings for some hungry patron. Sal was not the warmest of guys, so Mickey didn't bother greeting the man. He didn't need to hear Sal tell him to go fuck himself.

"Hey boys," Mickey greeted as he pushed open another door and walked into a much larger room that was strictly off-limits for bar staff.

"Hey Mickey," Dominic greeted as he raised his fist, waiting for a fist bump.

Dominic was one of the few Italians Mickey had working on his crew. While he was not Irish, Dominic knew the value of loyalty and family.

The truth was that Dominic was like family. He was only a year younger than Patrick and began following them around like a lost puppy when they were kids. The three of them spent evenings playing basketball at the local courts, getting into fistfights with the other hoodlums in the area, and chasing any young broad who batted her eyelashes in their direction.

When Dominic turned eighteen, Mickey and Patrick chipped in to get a hooker to pop his cherry. They later found out that Dominic's cherry had already been popped a year earlier by one of his mother's friends who had recently separated from her husband and needed a young, uncut piece of meat to keep her company.

Next to Dominic sat Thomas, an older man in his seventies who always had a constant scowl plastered on his face. Mickey wondered if perhaps the scowl became a permanent fixture on a man's face once he reached fifty. Even his father now had a constant resting-asshole face plastered to his ugly mug twenty-four seven. If so, he wasn't looking forward to aging.

"Is it true?" Dom asked with sadness in his voice.

Both men stared at Mickey, who froze just inside the door. He nodded his head.

"God damn!" Dom shouted, biting his fist in frustration.

"Watch your mouth, boy! Don't be takin' the big man's name in vain." Thomas was more religious than most of the guys on the crew when it came to attending church regularly or observing religious holidays. The man claimed to follow in the Lord's footsteps, but given the nature of what Thomas did for a living . . . was he really following the word of God?

"That was Beep's body they found this morning. He apparently fell off a roof or something. The police are investigating, so we should know more soon."

"Let me know what you need, boss. Day or night, just give me a shout," Dominic offered.

Everyone loved Beep, so his death would hit the crew hard.

"How about I set up a little drink thing at the pub one night with us and the boys to say goodbye properly?" Dominic offered.

"I think that would be a nice idea." Thomas said patting Dominic on the back, then resumed his counting.

Whatever the guys needed to help them heal, Mickey would provide it. Drinks sounded like a perfect way to send off Beep.

"So, how's it looking?" Mickey asked as he pulled a beer from the mini-fridge and took a seat at the small table the boys were gathered around.

"Not a bad hall," Dominic noted.

"Meh." Thomas scowled. "I'm pretty sure that prick on Eighth Street cut us short this week."

Mickey pressed his beer to the corner of the table and popped the cap off with his other hand. "What do you mean?"

The cold beer felt refreshing as it slid down Mickey's

throat. It was only June, but man, the days were starting to heat up.

Thomas held up a stack of cash and glared at the two men eyeing him. "Based on the quantity of coke we gave 'em last week, he shoulda given us fifteen thousand cash this week. He said he sold out, but he only gave us thirteen Gs this mornin' when we collected. So, either he didn't sell out and kept the extra coke for himself or the guy sold out but kept the cash. Either way, the dumb fuck is tryin' ta fuck us in the arse."

Dom and Mickey burst out laughing. There was something about hearing a scowling man say "fuck us the ass" that was hilarious.

Thomas glared at the two even harder.

"Or there is another option. The guy is a dumbass and can't do simple math?" Dom offered as he took a swig of his beer.

"Should we start givin' the dealers calculators, so they know how much change to give?" This was one of the few times Thomas tried cracking a joke and it seemed a bit unnerving.

They all held in their laughter.

Mickey nodded. This was his responsibility to straighten out. Pops had assigned him oversight of the street crew, so if there were any legs to break, he was the one who had to sign the order.

"I'll go speak with him tomorrow," Mickey responded

as he stood up from the table. "You boys going to load the cash in the bar's ATMs?"

"Yeah, that's the easiest way for us to clean this cash. Why go get cash from a bank when we can just reload the machines with this money?" Dom was Mickey's personal money launderer. He was brilliant at math and always found creative ways to launder their dirty cash. Reloading the bar's two ATM machines with their drug money was one of his latest ideas.

Dom had explained that if you place the dirty cash into the ATM, that money would be withdrawn by customers using the ATM in the bar. The customer's banks would then credit their ATM business account the amount of the withdrawal made by the customer, thereby settling the transaction and giving Mickey clean money in his account.

The boy was a genius.

♣ ♣ ♣

A few hours later, Mickey emerged from his office in the back of the bar and decided to enjoy a few drinks with some of the boys who had come in for an evening pint.

Mickey slid into the booth next to Patrick and waited for Gale to bring him and the guys another round.

The bar was beginning to fill up with the usual rowdy crowd of patrons. It was a Thursday night, so they often got some of the local college kids dropping in to blow off some steam.

"Did you go speak to your old man?" Patrick asked,

between gulps of his beer.

Patrick leaned his 6'1 frame against the back of the booth as he surveyed the crowd spilling into the bar.

A few of the regulars averted their eyes and tried not to make direct eye contact with Patrick. He had quite the reputation in Jersey, even the mention of his name had people trembling.

He was the guy Mickey and his father called whenever they needed to extract information from a less than willing individual. Over the years, Patrick had developed skills and methods of releasing information from people's mouths. Sometimes the methods he used would make even the hardened of men cringe.

While others feared Patrick, Mickey did not. Mickey knew the real Paddy. He knew the shy little boy who used to cry for his mother late at night. He knew the sweet and loyal friend who would rather give his right arm than see a child get hurt.

Under that tough and brutal exterior hid the soul of a lonely man. One that only wanted to be loved.

Focusing on Patrick's question, Mickey could feel his blood boil. Mickey hated his father with a passion. The man was a mean-spirited, bigot, who always found a way to blame all his troubles on Mickey.

Telling his father that perhaps someone was targeting and killing members of his crew was not something he was looking forward to doing.

Somehow, this would end up being his fault. Some lack of leadership or lack of oversight—any bullshit excuse to focus the blame onto him.

"Nah, I got busy and didn't have a chance to see the old man. I'll do it tomorrow." He would have to find some time in between beating that little shit's ass over on Eighth Street and checking in on the club to stop by and tell the old man what was going on.

Patrick placed a hand on Mickey's shoulder and gave it a reassuring squeeze. He knew better than anyone the strained relationship Mickey had with his father. In fact, Patrick had a similarly strained relationship with his own father.

This common hardship was one of the things that kept Patrick and Mickey bonded as best friends. Growing up together, they had been like brothers. Always looking out for one another, always there to support each other.

It got to the point where the two of them even began sporting the same hairstyle. It had started as a joke a few years back but had somehow morphed into a feeling of comradery. It somehow connected them as brothers and created a bond that only the two of them shared.

It was stupid, but they loved it.

Both men sported an undercut with the top of their hair slicked back against the center of their head resembling a mohawk. While they did not spike their hair, both had dyed it two-toned colors.

Mickey's hair was primarily black with a thick strip of

red running down the middle, while Patrick's was primarily black with a thick strip of blue.

As if matching hairstyles weren't enough, both had fiercely green eyes, which sometimes had people questioning whether the two were actually brothers. To Mickey's knowledge, they were not related. But with all the fucking secrets families kept, you never really knew.

Mickey's eyes scanned the room when he heard raised voices. It wasn't uncommon for the bar to be filled with loud, rowdy people, but these voices were filled with venom. Something was going on.

His eyes stopped when they caught sight of Ian and Brody—two of his fellow crew members—picking on a young man who appeared to be in his early twenties. The young man's back was to Mickey, so he couldn't see his face, but didn't recognize him as one of their regular customers.

Mickey tilted his head, trying to see what the heck was going on in his bar.

"I asked you what the fuck you're looking at, faggot?" Brody growled at the young man.

"At the moment, a neanderthal. One who clearly has never been introduced to a shower," the cheeky boy snipped back.

Mickey choked on his beer as he tried not to laugh. The man was right. Brody was not the most hygienic person around. Brody claimed that women loved his man stench, but Mickey was convinced the man was just lazy.

"What did you say to me, boy? I think it's time for ya to get your faggoty ass up and out of this here bar before I take you out back and make you my bitch," Brody growled, taking a step closer to the young man.

Mickey noticed the subtle shift in the boy's body. He had moved from a casual stance to a more defensive stance as if preparing himself for an attack by his aggressor. The boy was clearly terrified of Brody but was doing his best to put on a tough exterior while standing up to his bully.

It was like watching David and Goliath battle it out in his pub. Brody had a good sixty pounds of muscle on the young, slender twink standing his ground.

Mickey's eyes fell to the boy's right foot, which was nervously tapping the wooden peg on his chair. The poor guy.

He felt a sudden urge to protect the boy. Here was a young man, trying his best to defend himself and his dignity against a clearly superior opponent. All Mickey wanted to do was wrap his arms around the young man's delicate frame and protect him from the imbecilic meathead towering over him.

Mickey had enough. He placed his fingers between his lips and whistled loudly, catching Brody's attention.

Brody's body stiffened as he recognized his master's call.

Mickey simply shook his head from side to side, then pointed his thumb over his shoulder, indicating that Brody and Ian were to leave the bar. Now.

Brody's eyes were locked on his boss, appearing to have forgotten all about the snippy young man he was trying to intimidate. He gave Mickey a simple nod, acknowledging his boss' orders, then turned and walked out of the bar with his buddy.

At the bar, the boy looked confused as he watched his aggressive opponent suddenly leave the pub without a word.

A head of perfectly sculpted brown hair turned and glanced around the bar, searching for answers. Mickey did not react, only sat there, watching the boy in his confusion.

The guy was beautiful. His bold brown eyes scanned the room, seemingly looking for some explanation. His delicious lips moved to the side as frustration set in. He would get no answers to his questions today.

There was something about his delicate features that made Mickey's dick take notice. Perhaps it was the feminine quality of the gorgeous young man's features. Or perhaps it was the knowledge that under those soft elements lay a beast in waiting, willing to defend its honor against an opponent twice its size. His own "little tiger."

Whatever it was, Mickey was intrigued.

Unsure of what had just happened, the boy turned back to his beer and took a sip.

"Cillian," Mickey called out, signaling for Cillian to come to the table.

"Yeah, boss?"

"See that guy at the bar with the black T-shirt?"

"You mean the fag at the bar?" Cillian chuckled.

"Don't ever fucking use that word in this bar again, or I'll take ya out back and bash ya fuckin' head in," Mickey growled in a thick Irish accent. Even though Mickey was born in America, his accent always thickened when he got pissed off.

Cillian's eyes went wide as he shot a panicked look over at Patrick.

Patrick just smiled and nodded in support of his buddy.

"Ah, sorry, boss. My bad." Cillian swallowed hard, worried that he had just pissed off his boss and was now on the boss's shit list.

"Tell Gale that the young man's drinks are on the house for the rest of the night . . . and any other night he comes in here."

"Are you sure, boss?" Cillian asked, stupidly.

Mickey glared at Cillian. One thing you never did was question the boss. Ever.

"Shit. Sorry, boss. Right away."

Cillian was just about to run off when Mickey stopped him.

"And tell Brody that Patrick wants to see him later tonight. Tell him to stop by the club around eleven." Mickey glanced over at Patrick, who gave him a nod.

Mickey wanted Patrick to teach Brody a lesson. One that would leave him a few teeth short the next morning. Behavior like his would not be tolerated.

Was he doing this to teach Brody some manners? Or was he doing this to defend the boy's honor? Mickey wasn't quite sure, but he did know he wanted to inflict pain on Brody.

Cillian ran off toward the bar and whispered into Gale's ear. She looked over at Mickey and nodded in acknowledgment.

Mickey watched Gale give the young man a new beer and whisper something to him. The boy looked confused and seemed to argue with her. Gale simply shrugged her shoulders and handed him a shot of Jäger. It appeared that no matter how much the boy argued, he was not going to win his argument against Gale.

He felt his chest warm as he struggled to keep his lips from curling up in a smile.

"So, how bad do you want his lesson?" Patrick asked, bringing Mickey's attention back to the table.

"Knock out a few teeth, but don't knock the idiot unconscious. He still has a few runs for me to do tonight. Just make sure he understands I won't stand for that fuckin' behavior."

Patrick grinned. Sometimes Mickey wondered if Patrick got off on inflicting pain on others. Thank God he was on Patrick's good side.

Mickey watched his new fascination drink alone at the bar for the next two hours. Once the boy was done drinking, he spent ten minutes trying to convince Gale to charge him for the drinks. Once he realized his protests were useless, he shoved forty into a tip jar.

At least the boy seemed to have a decent heart.

Mickey watched as the boy thanked Gale and stumbled out the front door.

"Pass me your hat and hoodie," Mickey said as he reached over and yanked the hoodie out from under Patrick's ass.

Patrick didn't protest, only stared at him confused. "Where are you going?"

"I'll catch ya later tonight. Don't forget. Brody! Club!" Mickey shouted as he followed his new obsession out the door.

CHAPTER 4 - Seth

Seth stepped out of the pub and stumbled before he caught his balance. Okay, perhaps he had a little bit more to drink than he had originally intended. Damn Gale and her constant free beers and shots.

It didn't take Seth long to quickly realize that every time he asked Gale why he was getting free drinks, she always responded by handing him another shot of Jäger. A sure-fire way of avoiding the question.

Like Pavlov's dog, he eventually learned that asking that question, resulted in pain for his liver. It took a while, but eventually, he stopped asking and just enjoyed the free booze. Why question a gift someone had so clearly bestowed upon him?

The original plan was to have a few drinks in the bar while scoping out all the hot Irish dudes. He was hoping to locate a hot straight guy who leaned anywhere toward the right on the Kinsey scale.

A straight Irish dude with just a touch of homosexual curiosity was just what he needed. Straight dick with just enough aggression to make him sore for a week. He needed to get railed, and a random hookup was the perfect solution.

Fuck. It had been a while since he last got fucked and he was majorly craving some D.

Of course, the booze only amplified his need to get plowed hard and without mercy.

Shit. Perhaps having all those drinks was not a good idea.

Seth cut across the street and headed toward the subway. He lived only a few subway stops away but was too tipsy to walk the ten blocks back to his apartment.

The sun had set a few hours ago, and it was quickly approaching late evening. Seth glanced at his watch. It was almost ten. He debated. Did he want to go home?

He knew he probably should.

At that moment, his mind fell back on his encounter with the aggressive neanderthal he had met earlier.

The asshole had caught Seth checking out his crotch while waiting at the bar. In his defense, the guy had been scratching his balls in his gray jogging pants for the past five minutes. Men in gray jogging pants equaled Seth on his knees. That was his weakness. Well, it was most gay men's weaknesses.

Having the guy come at him so aggressively had scared Seth. He tried to act tough in front of everyone in the bar, but secretly, he was terrified the guy was going to knock his lights out.

The guy was fucking huge. His muscles were the size of Seth's thighs . . . well, not that Seth was a big guy anyway, but the point was the guy could easily kick his ass into the ground.

It got to the point where Seth had two choices: pretend to be tough and stand up to the guy—possibly resulting in his death—or cower in fear and never be able to hold his head high again in public.

He had survived his share of gay bashing and harassment when he was in high school. He didn't want to continue to live his life in fear, afraid to be who he was.

It was this anger that he clung to, hoping it would give him enough strength to take whatever beating the homophobic asshole was about to give him.

Seth wondered what it was that made the guy suddenly stop his barrage of hate-filled speech. Someone had whistled in the bar, the man froze, then suddenly left the bar, looking like a puppy that had just been kicked.

It was in that moment that clarity set in, and Seth suddenly realized why he had continued to drink so much. It was to drown out the humiliating feeling of helplessness he felt during his encounter with the angry homophobe.

Seth had spent so much of his childhood feeling helpless and small. Growing up as a gay kid was never easy for anyone. Constantly having to hide who you are, always afraid someone might discover you are attracted to men. Knowing that no matter how hard you tried, you could never turn off those feelings you weren't supposed to have.

No matter how hard he tried, he was constantly made fun of and harassed for his flamboyant tendencies.

He hated the feeling of being helpless and powerless.

He needed to feel powerful once again. His mind was made up. He wasn't heading home just yet.

Seth dodged two women exiting the subway as he jogged down the steps toward the platform.

The cool air from the arriving train splashed against his warm face as he waited for the train to come to a complete stop.

In typical New Jersey fashion, everyone rushed the doors when they opened, regardless of any little old lady trying to exit the train.

Seth found an empty seat by the window and popped his headphones into his ears. Fifteen minutes and then he would be at his destination—a place where he could regain his sense of power, a place where a twenty-two-year-old twink with a firm ass was always treated like a God.

In his excitement to get to his destination, Seth failed to notice the muscular Irish man who had followed him onto the train. The man now stood three rows back, watching Seth with hungry eyes.

Twenty minutes later, Seth entered Sebastien's Spa—a local gay bathhouse—and made his way to the lockers.

An evening at the spa was just what he needed to feel confident and powerful once again. Being desired by so many men, knowing that all of them wanted him and his tight firm body. That he had the power to choose which guy . . . or two . . . got the pleasure of enjoying his body for the night, always made him feel so empowered.

Given that he had spent the evening feeling like a powerless loser, he needed a major confidence boost and Sebastien's Spa was just the ticket.

"Hi, sexy," a furry cub in a jockstrap greeted as he walked past Seth in the locker room.

Seth nodded as he removed his shirt and threw it in the locker. A smile emerged on his face. He was feeling better already.

CHAPTER 5 - Mickey

He lowered the hoodie so his hair and eyes were obscured from the public. He stood in the shadows as he watched the young man open the door and head into the spa.

Part of him wanted to follow the boy inside and see what sort of trouble the sexy twink would get into. But another part of him wondered what the fuck he was doing here.

He had followed this guy, a paying customer, onto a subway, and now into a spa. What was he doing? He was pretty sure he had now officially crossed over into stalker territory. These are the things they talk about during TV documentaries. The creepy loner who followed the unsuspecting victim onto a train, then back to their home . . . or in this case, to a bathhouse . . .

He had no idea why, but he wanted to learn more about this mysterious creature. He wanted to be near him, observe him, admire him. He felt like a kid with a shiny new toy. It was his and he wanted to discover all its features.

But what if someone recognized him?

Who the fuck cared? It's not like anyone was going to have the guts to say something or stop him. He was next in line to run his father's criminal organization. They had police officers and judges in their pockets, and everyone in Jersey . . . Well, those who participated in the darker elements of society knew not to fuck with Mickey and his crew.

Mickey looked up and down the street. They appeared to be in one of Jersey's less popular gay areas. The likelihood of anyone recognizing him in this area was very slim.

Even if someone did, they would have to reconnect their jaw before they tried to tell anyone.

Fuck it. Mickey crossed the road and entered the Spa.

"Room or locker?" the balding man barked from behind the plexiglass without looking up from his phone.

"Just a locker," Mickey replied as he slipped the man a twenty.

The man passed him a towel and pointed him down a hallway. Mickey adjusted his hoodie and grabbed a handful of condoms from the tiny bowl on the counter. Hey, if they were free, why the fuck not?

Mickey was no stranger to sex clubs or bathhouses. He and the guys often frequented such establishments when out partying or on vacation. He was no prude when it came to sex and had a very high sex drive.

This, however, was the first time he'd come into a spa with the sole purpose of observing one person. He wasn't here to bust a nut or get his cock sucked. He was curious about the fierce tiger who had shown his claws earlier in his bar.

Even though the boy had been terrified out of his mind, the fierce little tiger still stood his ground and stuck up for himself. That showed a lot about someone's character. And people seldomly intrigued him.

The place was dark and smelled of poppers and sweat. He guessed the building had been here for at least fifty years as the walls and plumbing looked a bit dated.

Mickey pulled off his hoodie and shirt and tossed them into the locker. Next, he unzipped his pants and placed those into the locker as well.

He adjusted his red boxer briefs, then turned to face the full-length mirror next to the row of lockers. He checked out his muscular body, admiring each bulge and curvature.

His body was covered in tattoos he had collected over the years. He had a full-length sleeve that covered his left arm and shoulder as well as a large demon tattoo that covered the majority of his back. His favorite of all his tattoos was the large three-leaf clover that sat over his left chest muscle. Running behind the clover were an Irish and a French flag that crisscrossed each other. The flags represented his heritage—Irish for his father, and French for his mother.

His mother was a young French beauty named Sofia Devoiux, who happened to catch his father's eye when he was in his early twenties. From what Mickey remembered of his mother, she was a kind and loving woman. Sadly, his mother passed away when Mickey was only six, so he did not have many memories of her. His father refused to talk about his mom, so Mickey rarely asked.

Damn. He looked fucking ripped. He could give Marc Walburg in his Calvin Klein ad a run for his money.

Mickey grabbed his cock and gave it a bit of a squeeze as he admired his reflection. He pulled the ballcap lower on his head, shielding part of his features. Fuck the towel.

He tossed the towel into the locker and slammed the door shut.

"Damn, Papi, you look fit as fuck. Let me know if you want to take this fine ass for a spin," a slender Latino offered as he eye-fucked Mickey.

"I'm good, thanks," Mickey replied as he walked past the thirsty Latino and into the dark hallways of the spa.

All the rooms were dark as men used the shadows to hide their identities or play with their mates. The sound of men moaning and cocks slapping against flesh filled the air as Mickey walked deeper into the den of sin and debauchery.

There was something about the smell of sex and moans in the darkness that turned Mickey on. His cock began to swell in his boxer briefs as he hunted his prey.

Room after room, nothing but horny men enjoying themselves. There was no judgment here, just horny men looking for a quick release.

Then Mickey spotted him. The tiger from the bar. The boy was down on his knees sucking the dick of a large black bear while a muscular ginger played with his ass.

Mickey stepped into the darkness and watched the boy as he enjoyed the company of his two playmates.

From the darkness, Mickey's dick thickened. Watching the boy, with his perfect ass, swallow the man's huge cock all the way down to the base. Damn, the guy knows how to deep throat.

He reached into the front of his boxer briefs and pulled out his rock-hard cock. He couldn't remember the last time his dick had been this solid. Seeing that plump, juicy ass on full display made Mickey want to do very bad things to it.

He licked the palm of his hand and began rubbing the full length of his cock. He wanted to be face-deep in that sexy ass. The slurping sounds coming from the young man had Mickey gripping his cock even tighter. He pictured himself sliding his rod in and out of those swollen red lips.

From behind, Mickey watched as the ginger rolled on a condom and adjusted himself behind the young man's eager ass.

Mickey squeezed his cock tighter as he watched the ginger line his slick cock up against the twink's ass before starting to slowly push into him.

His little tiger let out a gasp as his body was invaded by the thickness of the ginger's cock.

Mickey studied the man's face as his expression changed from one of pain to one of ecstasy as he began taking the full length of the man's cock.

The image of the ginger was replaced with the image of Mickey, plowing deep into the young man. Hearing him gasp as he invaded his tight space made his dick thicken.

The things he wanted to do to that man . . .

"Oh, fuck me harder," the boy cried out in between moans. He grabbed the bear's cock and shoved it back into his mouth as he swallowed it whole once again.

Mickey watched the two men take advantage of *his* horny little twink. He didn't even know the guy, yet he had already claimed him as his own . . . What was wrong with him?

He felt his jaw clench as he thought about the two men invading the body of the scared, nervous young man he had seen at the bar. His scared little tiger with the ferocious bite. The boy he wanted to wrap in his arms and protect from the world.

Anger began to build as he watched the men use the boy for *their* pleasure. Neither seemed concerned with making sure the boy was being satisfied. Neither seemed to care that the boy's knees were turning red from the brute force of their activities.

If the boy belonged to him, he would always make sure his feisty man was taken care of. That his needs and his pleasure always came first. This did not mean he would not pound the boy hard into the mattress, he would just make sure that every thrust, every inch that invaded his body, always hit the boy's G-spot.

Mickey would make sure every orgasm ended with the horny young twink seeing stars and being unable to walk the next day.

Throbbing cock in hand, he thought about all the ways he would invade and worship his little tiger's body.

Jealousy began to rage as he watched the boy's ass continue to be invaded by the dumb fuck ginger who clearly had no idea where a man's prostate was.

Mickey could feel his balls tighten as his grip on his cock tightened. He watched the boy grab his own cock and begin jerking himself, a clear sign that he was not getting the pleasure he needed from either of the men fucking him.

Two minutes later he watched as the horny little twink threw his head back and shot his load all over the floor. That was all Mickey needed to go over the edge. He bucked his hips and shot his load into the darkness.

Fuck. That was a huge load.

Jealousy and anger continued to rage as Mickey watched the two men continue to enjoy the young man's body. The more he watched the more he wanted to beat those fuckers to a bloody pulp. Part of him wanted to leave before he went over and did something he shouldn't, but part of him needed to stay and make sure his little tiger was okay.

At that moment he watched as the ginger and then the bear shot their loads with a giant roar. The two gave each other high fives as they got up off their knees and left the room without a thought about the young man they were leaving behind.

The young man sat quietly on the floor, naked, staring at the cracks in the concrete. There appeared to be so much sadness in the young man's eyes.

Mickey took a step closer, trying to determine what he was thinking. Then he recognized the look in his eyes. Emptiness. The boy was feeling empty and alone.

Feelings Mickey himself knew all too well. All his life he'd felt empty and alone. Not being able to embrace who he truly was, was a huge contributing factor to that loneliness.

Being bisexual in an overly macho world did not come without its challenges. You were never able to speak openly about your feelings or dates. You were always having to hide one part of yourself. Never truly being able to open up to anyone or experience happiness and satisfaction.

Yes, Mickey recognized that look.

Mickey tucked his cock back into his shorts and watched as the young man put on his underwear and walked slowly into the locker room.

Being careful not to be seen, Mickey followed him and

watched as the young man showered, then dressed.

Throughout the whole process, his expression remained the same. There was no happiness or satisfaction. Yes, he had blown his load and felt a momentary sense of euphoria, but that high was short-lived and quickly lost when the realization of being alone set in.

Against his better judgment, Mickey hopped in a cab and followed the sad young man home. He knew he had passed "serial killer stalker" a few hours ago, but he needed to make sure he made it home safely.

For some unknown reason, he felt protective and needed to be sure the sexy young man who had captured his attention was okay.

CHAPTER 6 – Mickey

It was just after midnight when Mickey finally pulled up to The Lady's Touch, another one of Mickey's business ventures, also known as "The Club," to members of his crew.

The Lady's Touch was a strip club that Mickey had purchased about three years ago when he first started making some real money.

Dominic mentioned that it would be a smart move to purchase another bar or club to generate additional income and diversify his portfolio.

Yeah, diversify. The fuckin' wop actually used the word *diversify*.

Dom explained that the strip club would be a legitimate business that would generate legitimate money. Then, of course, Mickey could always throw in some of his own 'dirty' money and mix it in with the legitimate cash deposits into his company bank accounts. Since a strip club was mostly a cash-intensive business, it would be hard for banks and authorities to tell what money came from the legitimate business and what money came from any of their other illegal endeavors.

These days their illegal businesses mostly involved drugs or gun trafficking. Occasionally, Mickey's father would take on a special request job if it didn't impede his other business dealings and if the price was right.

The O'Briens used to be in the sex trade business as well, but a fucking Ukrainian gangster moved into Brooklyn and took over the market.

Mickey's father tried to take back control, but the Eastern European trash was way too powerful. His father even went so far as to hire a professional hitman to take out the fucker, but somehow Kos got wind of the hit and returned the hitman's head in a box.

Eventually, a truce was struck, and the Irish moved into the gun trade, leaving control of the sex trade to the Eastern European psycho.

As fate would have it, the psycho's network had been taken down about a year ago by what appeared to be a rival gang. Mickey and his crew were still trying to confirm which gang had taken him out before they attempted to reclaim control of the sex trade industry in their area. Mickey didn't want to put his men in the middle of a gang war if this group was just as crazy as the Ukrainian.

Better to be sure all the bullets had stopped flying

before you stick your head out.

Mickey walked into the club and bumped fists with Jake, the Hungarian beast of a bouncer, who stood next to the entrance of the club.

Jake was a walking advertisement for steroids. With muscles the size of bowling balls and a head shaved like an army sergeant, everyone feared Jake.

As he stepped further into the club, Rob Zombie's *Living Dead Girl* blasted over the speakers.

Mickey smiled. This was *her* signature song.

Angel.

The fiery redhead began dancing at his club six months ago. This woman was a walking sex goddess in six-inch heels. She was rumored to be dating Jake, but nobody had the guts to ask either of them. She would ignore the question, giving people one of her death stares, and Jake would smother whoever asked with his bicep.

The club was busy at this time of night. Mostly college guys and married men who preferred to motorboat fake titties than stick their dicks in their loving wives.

Mickey pulled a fifty out of his jeans as he walked past the stage. He nodded toward Angel, who crawled to the edge of the stage before she spread her legs wide open for him to deposit the cash in her . . . G-string?

Pussy or cock, it made no difference to Mickey. He secretly loved them both. While it was much easier to fuck women, from time to time, he did hook up with the occasional guy discreetly.

Angel closed her legs, securing his deposit before she flipped over on her knees and ran her tongue up Mickey's cheek.

Mickey burst out laughing. "Damn. You have a wicked tongue, sweetheart."

She gave him a wink as she turned back to the row of rowdy, horny men who were now making obscene gestures with their mouths.

Mickey signaled Jake and nodded toward the unruly bunch.

Jake nodded his head in acknowledgment as he made his way over to the group to gently remind them that women in G-strings needed to be respected.

It was like watching five young children suddenly realize that their father had just taken off his belt and was now headed their way. They all shrank in their seats and quickly pulled cash from their wallets, stuffing as many bills as possible into Angel's panties.

The sheer terror in their eyes made Mickey smirk. Not so tough now, are you, guys?

"Is he back there?" Mickey asked Starla, one of their more popular bartenders.

Her platinum blonde hair and perky fake tits kept the gents spending their hard-earned cash on drinks and lap dances.

"Yeah, he's been back there for about an hour now," she told him.

The back of the club was restricted and off-limits to most of the club staff. Only those with authorization or special permission were allowed in this area.

Mickey pushed open the large metal door that divided the club from the rooms in the back.

Just past the door and to the right, was Mickey's private office where he conducted business that not even his father knew about. To the left was another swinging door that led to a high-tech kitchen Mickey used to feed the guys.

Mickey himself never cooked, but there were wives and mothers of the crew who were always stopping by to cook up a batch of something to feed their growing boys.

None of the women seemed to care that they were stepping foot in a strip club. In fact, many of them had become friends with some of the dancers, sharing beauty tips and occasionally blow job techniques.

His crew was always well fed and taken care of.

Further down the hallway was a large steel door that led down to the basement. The basement was strictly off-limits to everyone except Mickey and his crew.

The basement, which had been reinforced with soundproof walls and barriers, was used for crew business. Business that was usually conducted by Patrick with unwilling participants.

This was Patrick's domain. Years of honing his skills

and making quite a reputation for himself made the basement his wonderland. A land filled with tools, contraptions, and gadgets that one could only guess how they were used.

Mickey pulled open the door and made his way down the metal staircase. The temperature in the basement was much cooler than upstairs in the club. Most nights, Mickey barely noticed the difference, but tonight he felt more sensitive for some reason.

The basement smelled of sweat and blood. Some of it fresh, some of it remnants from past interrogations.

Mickey approached the group of men who were gathered around watching Patrick work over some dude tied to a chair.

As he approached, his eyes fell on Brody, who was standing . . . well, rather teetering, next to Ian, pretending to watch the show. Brody's face was bashed up, and his lower lip was bleeding—clear signs that Patrick had his lesson with Brody.

A sense of pleasure settled in the pit of Mickey's stomach.

"How're we doin' here, boys?" Mickey asked as he approached the group.

Patrick stopped punching the man in the chair and took a step back. He wiped the sweat off his forehead and ran his arm along his sweatpants. His bare chest glistened as he turned to face Mickey.

"Just gettin' caught up with our friend, Akeil, here." Patrick walked over and grabbed a bottle of water off the table and began chugging.

The man in the chair sat hunched over as a long string of blood and drool made its way down to the concrete below.

"Judging by all the mess, I take it he isn't cooperating?" Mickey glanced around the room, taking note of the blood splatter and overturned furniture.

Patrick turned to face Mickey. "No. Some of that mess was thanks to Brody." He pointed his water bottle over at Brody, who suddenly looked sheepish. "Turns out he didn't realize that when he was told to come see me, that meant he was gettin' an ass-whoopin'."

Mickey glanced over at Brody, pissed. "He fought back?"

Patrick let out a laugh. "Nah, man. He thought I was playin' with him, so I broke a chair over his head. Then he realized why he was really here. After that, he took his beatin's like a man."

Brody looked up at Mickey with remorse in his eyes. "Sorry, boss. I won't use those words in the bar no more."

"Good to hear. Now, go get cleaned up and take the rest of the night off. You can finish your pickups in the morning." Mickey watched as Brody shook his head in thanks, then walked up the metal staircase still clutching his cheek.

"And this guy?" Mickey asked, turning his attention back to the man bleeding on his floor.

"Well, this guy is the cause of all this mess over here." Patrick pointed to a bloody brass knuckle, some clamps, and a bottle of salt.

"What's up with the salt?"

"Stings like a bitch when you place some in an open wound." Patrick finished off his water, then walked back to where the group was standing.

"So, what did you find out?"

"Apparently, Akeil was chilling with Beep up on the roof of that building most of the night. They were drinking beers and sniffing some coke. According to this dipshit, Beep offered him some purple powder shit he had never seen before, saying that he got it off a new dealer and that it was supposed to give you a wicked high. But since Akeil never heard of this shit and didn't know the dealer, he didn't try any of it.

"He said Beep snorted the shit, then a few minutes later Beep was losing his mind. Screaming that monsters were all around him and trying to eat his face. This dipshit said he got so freaked out he took off and left Beep alone on the roof.

"By the time he got down to the ground floor, Beep had already jumped off the roof and was dead on the ground," Patrick finished, glaring at the pathetic man slumped and tied to the chair.

Mickey turned to the man with disgust in his eyes. "You fuckin' left your best friend alone on the roof while he was trippin' on a bad batch of whatever the fuck that shit was?" Mickey was furious. There were certain things you didn't do to friends, especially when they were having a bad reaction. Leaving them alone on a roof was one of them.

The man's shoulders began to bob up and down as he continued to cry. "I know. I'm sorry. I never should have left Beep alone up there." The man lifted his head as tears streamed down his face. "You don't understand. Beep was losing his mind! I've never seen a man act that way before. I freaked out and ran. I fuckin' hate myself for it." He broke down and sobbed.

"I don't fuckin' care! We are family! We look out for one another! When one of us is in trouble, we man up and take care of them! You don't fucking run off and leave!" Mickey was raging. It took all of his self-control, not to take out his gun and shoot this sniveling piece of shit in the face.

He began pacing back and forth, seeing no other way. Finally, he turned back and glared at the pathetic excuse for a man. "You're done! You're done with this crew! I can't have people who don't look out for one another as part of my family."

Akeil kept his head lowered as his sobbing increased.

Mickey had enough of this piece of shit. He turned to Patrick. "Paddy, fuck this guy up. Show him what we do to guys who betray the family. Beep was our fucking brother. He deserved better than this piece of shit watching his back."

Mickey turned and headed toward the metal staircase. From behind he heard the painful screams of the man who had betrayed a member of his family. He knew he could not bring back Beep, but at least he could get the poor man some justice. Now, he just needed to find out what the fuck that purple powder shit was and who gave Beep the deadly substance.

Fuck. There was one phone call he had to make first. On second thought, he better make it a visit. His father would be pissed if Mickey kept this situation from him any longer.

Reaching into his pocket, he pulled out his cell and hit *Call* on his father's number. Clive didn't go to bed until at least 2 AM each night, so Mickey knew he would still be up.

As predicted, his father answered on the third ring.

"Hey, Pop, it's me. Mind if I pop by for a sec? Need to discuss something with ya."

Twenty minutes later, Mickey entered his father's four-bedroom home that he shared with his latest pump of the month. Mickey didn't bother trying to remember their names as Clive liked to keep a revolving door of women coming and going at his pleasure. Most women only lasted about three months before Clive tossed them out for another, younger model.

Clive escorted Mickey into the living room where he handed his son a whiskey, then flopped down in a leather recliner.

Mickey noted the lipstick-stained cigarette that had recently been extinguished sitting in an ashtray on the coffee table. A steady stream of smoke was still escaping the small portion of the cigarette that still burned. Next to the ashtray lay a small mirror with a line of coke spread down the center. Clearly, Mickey had interrupted the party.

"Where's what's her name?" Mickey asked, noting his father was dressed in a pair of boxer shorts and a tight New York T-shirt that hugged his bulging muscles.

His father scratched his small gut, then scratched his balls, before taking a sip of his whiskey. "Sent the bitch upstairs while we men discuss business," his father answered, not bothering to look up at Mickey.

Mickey was used to his father's male chauvinistic behavior. It seemed that since Mickey's mother passed away, his father has been trapped in the 1950s. According to Clive, men ruled the household, while women were only good for cooking, cleaning, and sucking dick.

This way of thinking pissed Mickey off. Women should never be treated as objects and had just as many rights as men did. Thankfully, only Clive and a few other 'old timers' still shared this mentality. Once these old fucks were gone, Mickey would be able to implement a new regime. A new way of thinking.

Since Mickey handled the majority of the day-to-day

operations, most people were lucky enough not to be subjected to his father's backward mentality and fucked-up views. He couldn't wait for the bastard to retire or take a long walk off a short pier.

"Okay, you're here, you got a whiskey, now tell me, what the fuck do you want?" This time Clive gave him the courtesy of looking up from his drink.

"Jasper died today." Mickey watched as his father lowered his glass and stared absently through the bottom of his glass.

"Was it an accident?"

"The same type of accident that happened to Sven and Bernard. That makes three guys who have died over the past few months." Mickey's eyes were locked on his father's as he waited for the accusations and criticism outlining how he had failed as a leader. How it was his job to keep his men safe. How he was too weak and incompetent to ever lead the O'Brien crew.

The silence was deafening.

Clive downed his whiskey in one shot, then threw the glass into the fireplace, shattering into a thousand pieces. "What the fuck is going on here? You're supposed to be protectin' these guys! Instead, you're sittin' around with your thumb up your arse while we lose money, lose business deals, and apparently, lose men."

Mickey glared at his father. This coming from a man who preferred to snort shit up his nose and bed women while Mickey kept the business running and made sure the community was taken care of.

He knew it was useless to interject or provide some sort of explanation. In his father's eyes, he was a failure and Clive was the only one fit to run the crew.

"So, what are you doing about this?" Clive growled as he got out of his chair to get himself another whiskey.

"I've got Patrick investigating this quietly. We don't want the crew to panic until we know exactly what's going on. So far, these all look like accidents and suicides, but there are too many coincidences for these to be just accidents." Mickey turned to face his father, waiting for him to return to his lounge chair.

"You think this might be murder?"

Mickey watched the thoughts in his father's balding head turn as he let him stew in them for a few moments.

"We don't know anything yet. Only suspicions. We want to keep this quiet until we know for sure. If word gets out, other gangs will think we are weak, try and move in on our territory."

His father's face tightened with the mention of his crew being weak. "Watch this one close and let me know the second you find out anything."

Mickey shook his head. That was enough talk for one night. His father knew, now he could get the fuck out of this place. "Sounds good, Pops. I'll keep you posted." Mickey stood to leave and almost choked on his drink when he spotted his father's latest play toy standing in the hallway with one tit hanging out of her bra.

The woman looked coked out of her mind. Mickey hated that his father didn't have any limits when it came to getting high. Mickey only used drugs recreationally, just enough to get a buzz on and feel good. What was the point of getting high when you couldn't remember a thing? Especially when you weren't even aware that your boob was hanging out in the open.

"Don't forget to bring the coke when you come up to bed," the drug-sniffing magician reminded Clive as she struggled to remain standing.

Mickey turned to face his father. "Nice one, Dad. Real keeper."

Clive snorted at his son's sarcasm. "Yeah, but she likes to swallow."

Mickey gave a disgusted look. He never wanted to imagine anyone swallowing his father's load. "Nasty. I'm out. Night, Pops." Mickey pulled the door closed behind him and jogged to his car.

What a fucking night.

CHAPTER 7 - Seth

The warmth of the afternoon sun fell gently against Seth's skin as he enjoyed a little downtime. It wasn't very often that he got a chance to just relax and enjoy the serenity around him. That was one of the problems with living next to the "city that never sleeps," and neither did the noise.

It was Sunday afternoon and Seth decided to enjoy a few hours lounging in the sun at Liberty State Park. He brought a blanket, a book, a backpack filled with snacks, and a few of his favorite vodka coolers to enjoy.

He had debated inviting Eve, but she was way too much energy for him to handle today. He just wanted a quiet afternoon to chill and relax.

Seth flipped onto his stomach and adjusted the blanket beneath him. He reached for his book and flipped it open to where he left off. He was reading *The Shining* by Stephen King and figured it was safe to read while the sun was still high in the sky. There was less of a chance of being grabbed by the dead twin girls during the day. Although that woman in the shower . . . she might be able to get you no matter where you are.

This was the life. He could get used to the warmth on his skin and the peace and quiet. Just as this thought passed through Seth's mind a shadow stepped over his body.

Annoyed, Seth turned his head upward ready to ask the jackass to step out of the sunlight when he saw Alex's smiling face shining down on him.

"What the—?" Seth blurted, startled to see the face of the innocent-looking man, who sometimes secretly scared the shit out of him.

"Heya, Seth!" Alex screeched as he stepped to the side, temporarily blinding him with the sun's sudden assault on his eyes.

One of Alex's little torments, no doubt.

Sometimes the guy could be a little vindictive. There was something dark inside him that seemed to be growing as time progressed. Marc, his fiancé, didn't seem to mind or notice.

Leaning upward, he noticed Marc standing next to Alex. Marc didn't look as cheerful as Alex. Then again, he never seemed to be cheery anyway.

Marc was the guy who sat silently in the corner, brooding during any social engagement. He was like a menacing beast who preferred to observe undisturbed from the shadows, and God help anyone who tried to challenge him or Alex.

"Can we join you?" Alex asked, making himself at home on the blanket and pulling a cooler out of Seth's bag. "Brilliant. I could use a drink." Alex popped the cap off and took a sip.

Seth sat up, making room for his uninvited guests. "You know, when I mentioned that I was going to hang out in the park today, that was not an invitation for you to come join me," Seth tried to sound annoyed, but secretly he was glad to have the company.

Alex and Marc were the couple he aspired to become. The bond and connection the two of them shared was inspiring.

Occasionally, they would make comments about their past or drop hints as to how they fell in love, but they always seemed hesitant to get into too much detail.

Seth got the impression they had shared some sort of traumatic experience that had only served to strengthen their love and adoration for one another. Either way, he liked being around them. They somehow made him feel safe and like he was part of a family or something . . . minus the brief period where Alex wanted nothing more than to murder Seth for thinking he was trying to steal his man.

Yes, Marc was hot in that I'm-secretly-a-serial-killer-who-will-knock-you-out-drag-your-body-back-to-my-basement-and-fuck-you-into-the-ground-all-night-long kind of way.

Perhaps Seth needed to get his head examined if he thought that was hot. But the thought of an obsessively jealous tough guy willing to protect him and fuck him until his eyes rolled into the back of his head somehow turned him on.

"Ouch. Words can hurt, *little one*, words can hurt." Alex winked as he pretended to be offended.

Marc joined them on the blanket and immediately placed his hand on Alex's thigh. That was Marc's way of telling the world that Alex belonged to him.

"Want a drink, babe?" Alex asked, offering Marc one of Seth's coolers.

"No, I'm good. Thanks."

"So, what brings you guys out to my side of the pond?" Seth took the cooler from Alex's hand and popped the cap.

"Oh! You brought olives and slices of salami!" Alex cried, pulling out the plastic container from Seth's bag.

Apparently, they were hanging out now.

"I need you to look into something for me." Marc passed Seth a large black folder. "Don't open it until you're back at your apartment."

Seth took the file and slipped it into his bag.

Seth was studying to become a private investigator and had done a few contract jobs for Marc in the past. Follow people around, take photos, gather some intel. He enjoyed it as it gave him a chance to use the skills he was learning, plus it gave him an excuse to hang out with Marc and Alex.

Last year, Seth gathered information for Marc on a deadbeat dad who was refusing to provide child support for his kids. He wondered what sort of low life he would be investigating this week.

"What's the scenario?" Seth asked.

Marc glanced at Alex, who gave him a slight head nod. It was crazy, how the two of them barely needed to use words to know what the other was thinking.

"I need you to gather info on some Irish thugs operating out of Jersey." There was something in Marc's expression that made Seth uncomfortable.

"Irish thugs?" Seth asked with a tilted head.

"Well, they are more like the Irish mob," Marc casually mentioned, raising his shoulders slightly, trying to lighten the mood.

"The mob? Are you crazy?" Seth whispered as if someone might overhear them.

The only people remotely close to them were busy chasing a frisbee down by the water.

"It's low-risk intel gathering. I just need you to go hang out in their bars and clubs, listen, see what people are doing, and let me know if you see anything suspicious. I wouldn't ask you to do this if there was any chance you would get hurt," Marc explained.

"Intel gathering. What are you hoping to find out?"

Seth's interest was piqued. While he was a little nervous about investigating the activities of the Irish mob, he was curious about what had Marc so concerned.

Marc glanced at Alex once again, but then thought better of it. "Look, I don't want to get into the specifics, but several of the Irish crew members have died under unusual circumstances over the past few months and I just want to make sure the deaths are not part of a retaliation for a murder that occurred last year."

Seth watched Marc's facial expressions. The man was a master at manipulation and had an impenetrable poker face. He could not get a sense of what it was that Marc was hiding, but he knew Marc and if he asked him to do something, then he knew he could trust him.

"And who do you think might be seeking revenge?" Seth took another sip of his drink and waited for Marc to answer.

"We think it might be a Ukrainian crime family seeking revenge for the murder of one of their commanders who was operating a human trafficking ring in Brooklyn."

Seth almost choked on his cooler. "What? How? What do you mean a human trafficking ring?" Seth's eyes were wide with panic.

This was some serious shit. He wasn't sure he wanted to get involved in this type of intel gathering. What if Marc was right and the crime family found out he was investigating them? He'd be a dead man.

Marc placed his hand on Seth's shoulder, trying to calm

him down. "Do you trust me?"

Seth stared into Marc's golden-brown eyes and understood what Alex saw in Marc. That reassurance that he would look after him and nothing bad would ever happen. That he was safe with him.

"Yes, I trust you," Seth replied, feeling some of the tightness leave his chest.

"The trafficking ring no longer exists, and neither does the one who ran it. All I'm asking you to do is hang out at these establishments as a paying customer and let me know if you hear anything. I'll do the more dangerous intel gathering myself."

Seth nodded.

Alex leaned forward and handed Seth a thick envelope filled with cash. "There's a thousand dollars in there for you to use for expenses and to pay for your drinks," Alex said as he popped an olive into his mouth.

Seth discreetly placed the envelope next to the black binder in his bag for safekeeping.

"Okay, now that business is out of the way, let's get down to the fun stuff. Seth. How are plans comin' along for Eve's bachelorette party? Did you decide what we're doing?" Alex asked, seeming happy to be done with the unpleasant business.

Marc rolled his eyes. It was clear that Marc was only going so he could protect what was his.

Alex and Seth had decided to throw Eve a bachelorette

party, but as it turned out, Alex was swamped with work so didn't have as much time to help plan out the activities. As a way to compensate, Alex offered to pay for the majority of the event if Seth could handle planning the event and making the necessary arrangements. Considering Seth's financial situation, he was more than happy with this arrangement.

Seth sat up straight and crossed his legs so he was face to face with his co-conspirator.

"First, we're starting with drinks and some hors d'oeuvres at my place. Just to warm up a bit. Then dinner at Le Grand Papa."

Le Grand Papa was a gay bar famous for its drag nights and two-dollar tequila shots.

"*Ooooh*, Eve is going to love that!" Alex exclaimed.

"Yeah, I spoke to the owner, and they are arranging for Eve to be pulled up on stage during the drag show." Seth smiled. "Then after the show, we are heading over to the Steel Rod to end the evening with strippers, cocks, and loads of shots."

Seth was proud of himself. For a "Junior Gay," he had planned a pretty spectacular homo bachelorette party.

Seth was pulled out of his celebratory congratulations by the sound of someone growling. He looked over at Marc, who didn't seem pleased with the latter part of the evening. Seth tried not to laugh.

"Well, Alex, I guess you and Marc are excused from

the later part of the evening," Seth chuckled.

"Like hell we are! I'm going to make sure my girl gets all the shots and dick slaps she wants during her bachelorette party." Alex turned to Marc. "Don't worry, stud. I will be sitting in your lap the entire night. I'm not letting any *working boy* go anywhere near my man!" This confession of jealousy and protectiveness seemed to warm Marc's heart.

He smiled at Alex. "Sure, I guess we can go to the strip club as well."

Seth admired the two of them. The way they protected one another and knew how to comfort each other gave him hope that one day he might find that same level of love and devotion.

The three of them hung out in the park for the remainder of the afternoon. In the end, Seth was glad for the company. If he was being honest with himself, sometimes Seth got lonely living in Jersey all alone.

He was still relatively new to New York and was working on establishing a network of friends. Eve, James, Alex, and Marc had become his closest friends in the city, and he was happy to be included in their close circle of friends. Even if he was the third wheel.

Everyone was coupled up, except for him and he was not looking to become part of a thropple. He didn't mind having threesomes. Lord knows he had participated in more than a few three-ways and orgies over the years.

There was something about the sexual freedom of

group sex that he found erotic and sometimes exciting. Though it was only fun when he was single and there were no emotional connections. The second feelings developed with a partner, Seth became a strict monogamist. There was no way he was sharing someone he loved with anyone else.

Seth had no issues admitting he was the jealous type. He believed in love and monogamy and demanded the same from any partner he dated. If after a few dates, Seth got the feeling the guy was only looking for an open relationship or seemed like the type of person who would fuck around behind his back, Seth cut the strings and walked away.

He wanted to be the one and only star of his boyfriend's fantasies, just as they were to him. If not, the relationship was not worth the effort.

By the time Seth returned home it was well past dinner. He made himself a salad and some tuna, then made his way to the living room.

Seth took a bite of the tuna and pretended he enjoyed the taste. The truth was, he was on a tight budget and needed to watch what he spent.

Marc had been great at providing Seth with a steady, part-time income doing odd-ball jobs for him while he was still in school. This meant Seth didn't have to look for a regular part-time job and could concentrate on his studies.

Seth needed to be able to do this on his own. It was the one-off expenses that really hurt him, like Eve's bachelorette party. No matter what, Seth always found a way to save for unexpected expenses.

One of the easiest ways was skipping breakfast and dinner a few times a week. This helped to put some extra cash aside for bills and socializing. Plus, consuming fewer calories helped to keep him looking slim and tight. You were only young once after all. May as well enjoy the tight body while you got it.

It was funny when he thought about it. Growing up in Chicago, he never had to worry about money or where his next meal was coming from. Seth's family came from money. His father was a very successful corporate lawyer running his own law firm with his best friend and fellow partner, Eric Bromson. His mother Isabelle was your typical socialite. She didn't need to work. She was beautiful and came from money.

Seth's grandmother, Clarisa Dubois, was loaded and living in Manhattan. She was one of the first wives of a major fashion designer back in Paris. When she divorced her husband—who turned out to be gay—she took her rather large divorce settlement and moved herself to the Upper West Side in Manhattan. She lived very comfortably off the income from her shares in his company.

Seth had not spoken to his grandmother since his falling out with his parents. He'd made it very clear that he wanted nothing to do with his parents and his family's wealth. He kept making up excuses as to why he couldn't visit his grandmother during holidays or special occasions. So far, he had successfully managed to dodge her questions.

He worried that involving his grandmother in their problems would only complicate the matter and he didn't have the heart or the energy to deal with his parents. Seth would do what was necessary to put himself through school and take care of himself.

As he swallowed a mouth full of lettuce, he opened the black folder Marc had given him and sifted through newspaper articles and notes Marc had previously made.

He turned on the iPad Marc had given him and compiled his own notes.

Marc was right. There had been a total of three deaths in the last two months, with the last occurring just the other day.

The first crew member had died by running into oncoming traffic; the second had shot himself in the head; the third guy had decided to take a dive off the roof of a building. Each of the deaths appeared sudden and at the hands of the individual.

Strange.

Seth leaned back and rested his head against one of the pillows. Would a hitman take the time to make all these deaths look like suicides? What would have provoked all these men to take their own lives?

The wheels in his head began to turn.

CHAPTER 8- Seth

Seth spent the next few days combing through the information packet Marc had given him as well as conducting a bit of his own research. Seth needed to understand everything he could about the three victims and how the O'Briens ran their network.

The head of the Jersey crew was Clive O'Brien. He was forty-eight, married once to a French woman who died in a car accident over twenty years ago. Clive had one son, Michele O'Brien, thirty-one, who goes by the name Mickey.

The crew had been operating in Jersey since at least the early 1940s in one form or another and it appeared they operated similar to the Italian mafia in New York.

Their loyalty was to the family and their people; they looked out for Irish families and businesses mostly in and around the Jersey area. Their major source of income came from drugs, gambling, and running guns. For a brief period, they seemed to have the market on prostitution, but that income stream seemed to have stopped approximately ten years ago.

The crew owned dozens of properties, both industrial and commercial; everything from abandoned factories, storage units, bars, and carwashes.

Seth suspected some of these properties were probably used as fronts to conduct their less than legal activities and launder their dirty money. You needed cash-intensive businesses if you wanted to move large amounts of cash, and something told Seth that drug dealers probably didn't deal in electronic fund transfers or credit cards.

During the day, Seth scoped out these properties, being careful to remain undetected. The last thing he wanted was to get on someone's radar.

Each night he would return home and update his notes, mapping out the crime network and all its affiliates. He had also begun mapping out the personal profiles of each of the crew members.

Marc had taught Seth that if you truly want to understand how someone operates, you need to understand who that person is and how they think. Had the person suffered some sort of trauma as a child, causing them to be more cautious and less trusting of people they did not know? Did the person have any loved ones with special needs or illnesses? This often led to the person being more loving and patient, more open to listening. Or this factor could be used against the person as leverage if they ever needed to apply pressure or exploit a weakness.

Marc's lessons were insightful, but sometimes could be dark and disturbing.

Once, out of curiosity, Seth tried looking into Marc's past but stopped when he found out that Marc's mother had died of cancer when he was just a child, and his father had been an abusive drunk.

Tragically, or by some miracle, Marc's father died in a house fire when he was only fifteen years old. Having no other family, Marc was taken in by his best friend's family, the Sanders. As in Alex Sanders, his current fiancé. That explained why Alex and Marc were so close. They had gone through so much together their whole lives.

To this day, Seth never mentioned his research into Marc's past. He felt too guilty. Like it was somehow an invasion of privacy and breach of trust. He figured that whenever Marc felt comfortable with sharing his past, he would.

When it came to personal profiles of the crew members, Seth had lots of info on Clive O'Brien and several of the lower-level members but was finding it difficult to find much information on Clive's son, Mickey, and his best friend, Patrick O'Maley.

When it came to Patrick, Seth knew he had been extremely close with Mickey since they were kids and that Patrick appeared to be the crew's enforcer. Clive used Patrick to extract information from difficult people.

When it came to Mickey, Seth knew even less. The

man was next in line to take over when his father croaked and apparently owned a strip club. Seth could not tell if Mickey had a wife or a girlfriend or even where he lived. The guy was a pro at keeping his life secret.

Seth needed to gather more intel. He had gathered a lot of information on the structure of the organization, how it operated, and what sort of assets it held.

To be honest, he was pretty sure the NYPD would love to get their hands on this information. Depending on how things turned out, that might be an option.

Now, Seth needed to dig deeper and start making connections. Connections between the players on the field and activities in the background. Was there something suspicious with the three men who had killed themselves? Were they victims of some larger plot for revenge? Or were they simply just victims of an unhappy and stressful life?

If the latter ended up being true, then Seth had wasted a lot of time and effort documenting the organizational chart of a criminal organization.

Seth glanced at the clock that hung in his tiny kitchen. It was getting late. Time for him to head out for some more sleuthing in the back alleys of Jersey's seedy underworld.

Surprisingly, Seth felt his dick twitch.

Was all this criminal activity secretly turning him on? Perhaps, he should lock that terrifying question away for some future therapy session he was bound to need by the time he was thirty.

CHAPTER 9 – Mickey

The wretched sound of a cellphone ringing jerked Mickey from a deep sleep. For a moment he lay there, confused, unsure of what had pulled him from his slumber. Then his eyes jerked open when the damn thing went off again.

He let out a breath and rolled over to grab his cell phone. The digits on the screen read 2:25 AM. What the fuck was someone doing calling him at this god-forsaken hour? Someone had better be dead or bleeding.

Actually, come to think about that, he hoped no one was dead. That would not be a good thing to wish for.

"What?" Mickey barked into the phone. It was Patrick's number calling, so he knew it must be important.

"Is that how you greet all your loved ones?"

"Only the ones who wake me in the middle of the fuckin' night. What do you want, dickhead?"

"I need you to come down to the club. The boys caught someone sniffing around the club and warehouse."

Mickey's eyes shot open. Who the fuck?

"I'm on my way now to the club to question the prick. Figured with everything going on you'd want to know."

Patrick understood how Mickey liked to run his crew. Even though his father was still the official head, Mickey was the one who oversaw the day-to-day operations.

"Yeah, you're right. I'll be right in. Don't start without me." Mickey hung up and turned on the lamp next to the bed.

Beside him, two naked bodies stirred as the light disturbed their peaceful slumber.

Oh, right. He'd forgotten he'd had a little party last night after he left the club.

Mickey slapped the man's bare ass hard, laughing as the man jerked up with a growl. The woman laying tits up under the man's arm gave a yelp, startled by the man's sudden movement.

"Time to get up! Party's over," Mickey called, jumping out of his king-size bed and throwing on his boxer briefs.

Mickey tried to remember their names but couldn't recall for the life of him. They were apparently a young couple visiting from California who had stopped into the strip club for the show.

The woman had approached Mickey and asked if he

was interested in having a threesome with her and her husband. Apparently, her husband loved to get fucked by a guy while he ate her pussy. Mickey was horny and happily agreed to the offer.

The couple hastily threw on their clothes, still half asleep. The man rubbed his ass cheek as he walked past Mickey.

"Thanks for the hot three-way," the woman said as Mickey closed the door behind the couple.

He snorted at the comment. The sex was all right. It scratched an itch and got him off, but it was not on his top-five fuck list.

Twenty minutes later, Mickey was walking into the strip club and descending the metal staircase.

The whole drive over, Mickey was trying to think of who could be sniffing around his units. Was it a rival gang? Some druggies looking for a quick score? The police? Or was this connected to whoever was hunting them down?

He'd never really thought of it that way before. That someone might actually be hunting them down, one by one. But if they were, why make it so subtle? Usually, rival gangs came in, guns blazing, making a show of things as a warning to others who might be questioning their power.

He didn't like questions, and he hated not knowing things even more.

Patrick was sitting at his worktable, leaning back with his feet propped up as he wiped down the blade of a large hunting knife.

Mickey wondered if this was all part of an intimidation tactic he put on for the boys, or if perhaps this was something that calmed Patrick and gave him pleasure. Sometimes, Mickey wondered about his best friend's state of mind.

The muffled sounds of an angry voice rang through the basement. Mickey's eyes fell on the figure tied to the same chair that had held Akeil only a few nights before. The man's hands were bound behind the chair and there was a cotton hood placed over his head. Judging by the muffled sounds, Mickey assumed the man's mouth had been taped.

The soundproof barriers in the basement had a way of making people's voices sound somewhat unnatural in the open space.

Shout all you want, no one will hear you.

Mickey walked to where Patrick sat bored out of his mind.

"Hey, Paddy. So, what the fuck happened?" Mickey was pissed that his sleep had been disturbed and even more pissed that someone had been snooping around his shit.

Patrick tossed the knife on the table and began pouring two glasses of whiskey. He passed one to Mickey and downed the other. "Ian said he caught this guy taking pictures of the back of the club. At first, he thought the guy was just some perve trying to catch a glimpse of some naked tits, but then he said he recognized him having drinks at one of the other bars. When Ian looked through the pervs camera, he found a bunch of pictures from our other properties, including the warehouse, so he brought him in." Patrick passed Mickey a digital camera with a telephoto lens attached to the end.

Mickey took the camera and scrolled through the images. There were photos of the inside and outside of this club, exterior shots of his commercial properties, and the carwashes. The fucker even had shots of some of the homes belonging to some of the lower-level members of his crew.

Who the fuck was this guy?

Mickey looked up at Patrick, who didn't look impressed with the amount of shit this guy had documented.

"Who the fuck is this guy?" Mickey asked, his jaw tightening.

"Haven't asked yet. Been waiting on your slow ass."

More muffled shouts came from the angry man bound to the chair. He moved his body violently against the ropes, trying to free himself. The guy had fight in him.

Ian punched the guy in the face as he struggled against his binds. Mickey watched as the man's body slumped to the side and his chest began heaving while his shoulders began bouncing. Was he crying?

"Don't," Mickey called, as Ian's fist rose, preparing to deliver another mighty blow to the man in the chair. "That's Paddy's job."

Patrick smiled and stood up from his chair. He took

another shot of whiskey, then walked to where the crowd of crew members was waiting impatiently next to their captive.

"Let's see who's hiding under the mask, shall we, Scooby?" Patrick mocked, making a reference to the late sixties children's cartoon.

Mickey leaned against Patrick's worktable, arms crossed against his chest as he waited for the big reveal.

Patrick pulled the hood off the man's head and yanked the tape off the captive's lips with no finesse.

He really did seem to get off on inflicting pain.

"Ow, fuck!" the man shouted. "You didn't have to yank so fucking hard, you muscled douche bag!"

Mickey jumped to his feet, instantly recognizing that furious voice.

"Shut your mouth, punk, before I dislocate your jaw," Patrick snarled.

"Jesus, someone has anger management issues. Did someone not get enough hugs from his momma as a child?"

Mickey rushed over to Patrick's side and grabbed his arm seconds before Patrick knocked the mouthy little shit out. One thing you never mentioned was Patrick's mother.

"Whoa, easy, Paddy. No need." Mickey stared into Patrick's eyes, showing him he was serious.

Patrick unclenched his jaw and nodded.

Mickey took a deep breath to prepare himself. The last time he had seen this captive, he was on all fours getting pounded by a ginger.

The room was silent as all eyes fell on Mickey. Mickey never got in the way of Patrick when he was interrogating a guy. Mickey had his role to play, and so did Patrick. Mickey stepping in as he did was huge.

Slowly, he turned to face the fuming body in the chair. "What's your name?" Mickey asked with no emotion in his voice.

"None of your fucking business."

Mickey let out a chuckle. "Is that the way it's going to be?" The young man glared at Mickey, refusing to show any fear or weakness.

Mickey knew how to read people. He could smell the fear on the boy, no matter how hard he tried to mask it with his harsh words and sharp tongue, Mickey knew it was there.

The room was silent as all eyes watched Mickey stalk toward the mouthy shit tied to the chair.

He bent down so his face was inches from the boy's. "I've got ways of making you talk," his voice was nothing more than a chilling whisper. He watched as fear crept into the boy's eyes.

With his left hand, he slowly reached down into the young man's back pocket and pulled his wallet from his jeans. He listened as the boy nervously swallowed. The boy smelled so fucking good. Like vanilla and coconut.

Mickey opened the wallet and pulled out his New York driver's license. "Seth Richards. Twenty-four years old. Lives in Jersey. Likes to drink shots of Jäger." Mickey glanced at Seth to gauge his reaction.

"What? It doesn't . . . wait . . . were you . . ." the boy looked confused and flustered.

Mickey watched his sexy lips twitch as he struggled to find the words. Secretly, Mickey wanted to bite down on that quivering lower lip and see how it tasted.

Mickey cut Seth off, "So, tell me, Seth, what were you doing lurking behind my club and why were you snapping all those photos?"

He didn't want the others to know he had seen Seth drinking in the bar the other night. The night he gave Seth a lifetime of free drinks and gave Brody a decent beating for running his mouth.

Seth glanced at the room full of thugs, each patiently waiting their turn to beat into his face. "Umm, I can't tell you that."

The guy was dressed in black jeans and a dark green T-shirt; hardly the uniform of a drug dealer or an assassin. Was he perhaps working with the police? Was he a spy for whoever had taken out Kos' crew? Were they coming after his crew next?

He needed answers, but one thing was certain, he was not letting Patrick anywhere near this boy. This boy was his. His *little tiger*. His to protect. His to extract information from however he saw fit.

"I'll ask you again. Who are you working for?"

Mickey caught the way Patrick's body shifted. The others may not have noticed, but Patrick did. Patrick knew Mickey was holding back and for some reason was handling this kid with padded gloves. Patrick knew Mickey too well. At least Patrick had enough loyalty, not to say anything or question Mickey's actions.

He stared into the boy's chestnut eyes. They contained so many emotions: anger, contempt, hope, fear . . . and was that loneliness he saw?

If the eyes were the windows to our souls, then this boy had one hell of a complex soul.

Mickey realized there was only one way to get the answers he wanted. And standing in a room full of intimidating thugs was not one of them.

"Untie him," Mickey commanded, nodding to the two men standing closest to the chair.

Both men stared at him, confused.

"Are you sure, boss?" Ian asked.

Mickey's nostrils flared. "You heard me, untie him! And don't ya ever question my orders again. Are we clear, ya dumb shite?"

Ian jumped forward and began untying the boy. "Yeah, boss. Sorry, meant no disrespect."

Seth's face suddenly went white as Ian began untying him. Fear and panic filled his eyes. "No . . . I . . . please . . . " was all Seth could muster.

"Come with me." Mickey nodded toward the staircase.

Seth didn't move. He sat firmly in the chair, shaking.

It dawned on Mickey. The poor kid probably thought he was being dragged out back to be shot. His heart suddenly plummeted in his chest at the realization that he had caused such fear and panic in this poor boy.

Mickey walked to the chair and grabbed Seth by his arm, pulling him up to his feet. Mickey needed to save some face in front of the guys. He couldn't show weakness. But he also couldn't stand the terrified look of fear he was causing.

He pulled Seth toward the staircase, tightening his grip around his arm.

"No, please! Don't kill me! I swear, I'll tell you what you want to know!" Seth pleaded as he tried to pull himself free from Mickey's grasp.

The level of panic in Seth's voice sent stabbing pains to his heart. All he wanted to do was wrap his arms around this terrified young man and shield him from all the pain in the world.

Mickey pulled Seth toward him and whispered, "Listen, kid, I'm not going to hurt you. But if you want to get out of here alive, you need to calm down and do as I say."

The tension in Seth's arm softened as the boy turned to face him. "What?" his voice was soft and confused.

"Trust me, kid. I'll never hurt you."

There was a sudden shift as the boy somehow seemed to be comforted by these words. He stopped struggling against Mickey's pull and allowed himself to be led away.

Mickey grabbed the camera and Seth's bag off the table and headed up the metal stairs as quickly as possible.

Seth remained silent as Mickey led him through the kitchen and out the backdoor that led to private parking behind the club.

"Get in," Mickey barked as he shoved the boy's bag and camera back into his arms.

Seth's mouth dropped open as Mickey opened the door to his cherry-red MC20 Maserati.

"Holy—is this yours?" Seth gasped, still in shock by the sports car parked in front of him.

"Yeah, get in the fuckin' car," Mickey snapped as he ducked down into the driver's seat.

A moment later, Seth climbed in, completely in awe of the sleek black and blue leather interior. Mickey noted the gasp that escaped Seth's mouth the moment the engine came to life, and the interior was illuminated in soft blue lighting. It seemed Seth had suddenly forgotten all about the danger he was still in.

"Buckle up, sweet cheeks," Mickey said as he jammed

the gear into drive and sped out of the parking lot.

Seth let out a squeak as he grabbed the seatbelt and jammed it into the clip.

They sat in silence as Mickey pulled out onto the main road and sped off into the darkness.

From the corner of his eye, he watched as Seth played nervously with the lining of his bag. He wasn't sure what to say, or how to start a conversation. There were so many things he wanted to know about the young man sitting next to him. Where to begin?

"Are you taking me down to the river to dump my body?" Seth asked quietly as he stared at the road ahead.

Mickey thought he saw a tear form in the corner of the boy's eye. Shit—this guy really did think he was taking him someplace to kill him. His heart sank once again. "No, I'm not gonna kill you. I promised ya I would never hurt you."

"Yeah, but you're a sexy, badass gangster. You lie for a living."

Mickey couldn't help but chuckle. "So, you think I'm sexy?"

Seth turned, mouth hanging open. "Out of all that, that's what you heard?"

Mickey shrugged his shoulders as if disinterested. Inside, he was smiling. "Relax, kid, I'm taking you home."

"But you don't even know where I live."

There was so much suspicion and confusion in his eyes.

"Eight sixty-three Clarence Street, apartment four-oh-five, Jersey," Mickey replied as he made a right at the intersection.

"How? How do you know that?" Seth sat in shock, then it seemed to occur to him. "You read it on my driver's license. By the way, where is my wallet, you thief?" Seth pulled open his bag and rummaged through its contents.

Yes, Mickey had read the address on Seth's driver's license, but he also remembered the address from the night he followed him home. But he was not telling Seth that bit.

Mickey grinned at Seth's last comment. "You're calling me a thief? Didn't I catch your ass illegally surveilling my properties? Stalking my crew? What does that make you?"

Seth sat silently and stopped rummaging through his bag.

"I got your wallet in my back pocket. I'll give it back when we arrive. You can call me Mickey by the way."

Seth ignored him and continued to watch as they sped by traffic. He propped his arm on the side of the door and leaned his head against his hand. He flinched the moment his jaw touched his hand. "Damn."

Seeing the boy in pain made Mickey's heart sink once again. He felt terrible, like he had somehow let the boy down. He had failed to protect him and allowed him to get hurt.

"I'm sorry one of my men hurt you. If I had known that was you under that hood, I wouldn't have let anyone near you." Mickey placed his hand on top of Seth's and gave it a gentle squeeze.

Seth recoiled in fear.

Mickey tried not to take Seth's reaction personally. The poor guy had been tied to a chair and beaten. Plus, he had no idea who Mickey was and whether he could be trusted.

"Was that you who told the bartender to keep giving me drinks all night?" Seth turned slowly to face Mickey. His eyes were unsure as he proceeded with caution.

He was guessing Seth left the free drinks in his bar out of the question as a way to test Mickey. To see if he was really the one who had given him a blank check to the bar.

"And what happened to that guy's face? The one standing off to the side. He didn't seem too pleased to see me." Seth tried not to smile as recognition set in.

"Brody?" Mickey looked over at Seth and gave him an evil grin. "I asked Paddy to have a little one-on-one with Brody to remind him that homophobic slurs and harassment will not be tolerated in my bar or on my crew."

Seth's smile spread from ear to ear. "So, you basically defended my honor."

Mickey chuckled once again. "Well . . ."

He came to a stoplight and watched as an elderly woman crossed the road. He nearly jumped out of his skin when he felt Seth's hand suddenly on his.

"Thank you." Seth squeezed Mickey's hand as he turned his attention back to the road in front of them. "No one has ever stood up for me like that before."

Mickey waited, expecting Seth to pull his hand away. When he didn't, Mickey slowly pulled his hand out from under Seth's and placed it on top of his.

He liked being the big spoon, even if it was only holding hands.

"It was my pleasure." Mickey gently caressed the young man's hand with his thumb as they continued to hold hands for the rest of the drive home.

CHAPTER 10 – Seth

The entire time, Seth's heart was racing. He was alone in a car with the number two boss of the New Jersey Irish mob. While the sexy, chiseled hunk sitting beside him claimed he had no intention of hurting him, could he really trust a criminal at his word?

Seth knew law-abiding men who defended justice who couldn't be trusted. One such man was the reason he no longer spoke with his parents. Yet here he was, holding hands with this smoking hot piece of beef, trusting he was not going to be found floating face down in the Hudson River tomorrow.

Perhaps he should call Marc? Let him know what had happened and who he was with. At least then if he went missing someone would know who did it. Although, he had a feeling Mickey would be the one found face down in a river if he called Marc. There was something dark and scary behind those sullen eyes of Marc's. It was as though he secretly wanted to set the world on fire and watch it burn.

Seth couldn't believe he was still holding the man's hand. He had meant to pull his hand away after thanking him, but for some reason, his body refused to listen to his brain. And then when Mickey placed his large, rough hand over the top of Seth's, his heart stopped in his chest.

He was both insanely turned on and terrified at the same time. At the moment, this scary, hunky man seemed calm and not a risk to his health, but what happened if he moved his hand and ended up pissing the man off? Was it better to continue holding this man's hand and pray Mickey's mood didn't change?

But he kind of liked holding this scary dude's hand. There was something soft and caring behind those scary green eyes.

Seth decided to not overthink things and just enjoy the moment . . . no matter how intensely insane it was.

"Thanks for the ride," Seth said when they finally arrived at his beat-up apartment building.

He was just about to reach for the car door when Mickey's hand grabbed his thigh.

"Not so far, sweet cheeks. I'm coming inside," Mickey said.

Seth's head spun around. "What? Why?"

"We still have lots to talk about. Plus, I'm not sure I'm done with you quite yet."

There was something about the way Mickey was looking at him, coupled with the man's sexy accent that made his dick take notice. Was it possible to want to fuck someone who scared the shit out of you?

Mickey grinned and turned off the engine. It was as though Mickey had somehow heard Seth's thoughts and was pleased.

Seth exited the car and dragged his heels toward the elevator. As he watched the numbers in the elevator light up, he suddenly realized that this walking wet dream was about to walk into his shitty-ass apartment and see the pathetic squaller in which he lived. Fuck. For the first time in his life, he felt embarrassed about his home.

He didn't care if Eve or Alex saw his run-down apartment, they knew he was a starving student, and this was the best he could afford.

But he was about to let a man who drove a fucking Maserati into this shit hole. The man was going to take one look, then run home to get fumigated.

Actually, perhaps this might not be such a bad thing. His shitty-ass apartment might be the one thing that kept him from being murdered.

The elevator stopped on the fourth floor and Seth held his breath as they exited. These might be the last steps that he ever took . . . Then Seth took notice of the wallpaper that lined his hallway and all his thoughts of being murdered by the prince of the criminal underworld left his brain.

Had this wallpaper always looked so bad? He had never

noticed the rough state of the hallway. He liked it better when he was blissfully ignorant.

Seth unlocked his door and let Mickey step in first. "Sorry about the mess." He followed Mickey into his apartment and locked the door behind them.

He watched as Mickey slowly stepped around his tiny apartment, nodding his head. "Not bad. Reminds me of a place I used to have when Paddy and I were just wee lads."

"Is Paddy your boyfriend?" Seth asked, a little disappointed. If this hot stud was gay, of course he would have a boyfriend. He probably had several.

Mickey stopped in his tracks and looked at Seth. "No, no. Paddy's my best friend. We grew up together. He's like a brother to me."

Seth noticed that Mickey masterfully avoided answering whether he was gay or straight. Damn.

"And Paddy is Patrick, that guy who was about to detach my jaw from my face when I mentioned his mom?"

Mickey gave a wicked grin. "Well, yeah. Ya talked about his momma."

Seemed like a bit of an overreaction, but what do you expect from testosterone-filled thugs?

Mickey flopped down on the couch and threw his arm over the backrest.

"Make yourself at home," Seth said sarcastically as he walked into his kitchen. "Want a drink?"

"I'd love a whiskey if ya have any."

Seth shook his head. Who does this guy think I am? "I've got cheap beer, milk, or water. Which do you prefer, Al Capone?"

Mickey chuckled from the living room. "Cheap beer is fine."

When Seth returned to the living room, Mickey was sitting on the couch shirtless, flipping through one of Seth's textbooks.

"Here." Seth passed the beer and took a seat next to him on the couch. "Did you spill something on your shirt?"

Mickey looked up at Seth confused. "What?" Then he realized Seth was referring to his bare chest. "Oh, no. Force of habit. Normally I don't wear a shirt when I'm at home."

"But you aren't at home. This is my place," Seth stated the obvious.

Mickey smirked. "You telling me that you don't like staring at this six-pack and these pec muscles? Please. I can practically see your dick getting hard already."

Seth's face flushed red. He was focusing so hard on not popping a boner, but shirtless Mickey was proving too much to handle.

His eyes moved from Mickey's perfectly sculpted six-pack, up to his bulging pec muscles. The full sleeve tattoo and the three-leaf clover etched over his left chest muscle were too much for Seth's body to handle. There was even a tiny barbell nipple ring in his right nipple that sent Seth reeling.

He gave up trying to fight the blood rushing to his dick and just let it happen. The man already knew Seth was gay, so why would he be shocked if he popped a boner in front of him?

As if sensing his loss of the battle, Mickey smirked and took a swig of his beer. He had won this round. "Now, tell me who you are, and why are you investigating my crew," Mickey's words were so matter of fact that they caught Seth off guard.

Perhaps that was why Mickey had taken off his shirt, to throw him off balance. The fucker. Seth's eyes narrowed as he tried to figure out Mickey's game. Was he trying to seduce him, or just keep him distracted?

"The faster you start giving me answers, the faster we can get to the more fun part of the evening."

Holy fuck! What? Was he suggesting what he thought he was?

"Focus, kid. Who are you, and why are you investigating my crew?"

Seth finally gave up trying to figure things out. "Fine. I'm currently a struggling student as you can tell from the lovely palace I live in. I do freelance work for a friend of mine, and he asked me to take a closer look at your crew to see if there is a connection between the three crew members that died over the past few months."

Mickey stopped drinking his piss beer and his jaw

tightened. "What do you know about the guys that died? And who is your boss?"

Judging by the sudden coldness in Mickey's voice, Seth wondered if he might be walking on thin ice.

"My boss is a private citizen. He's worried that perhaps these deaths are part of a revenge plot against your crew." Seth was getting nervous.

He still feared Mickey and didn't know what words might set him off. If Mickey got pissed, there was no way he would be able to defend himself against someone so strong. Mickey outweighed him by at least sixty pounds of lean muscle.

"What sort of revenge?" Mickey's eyes were burrowing a hole into Seth's body as he spoke.

Clearly, Mickey was upset with the deaths of his mates, and the suggestion that perhaps their deaths had something to do with seeking revenge seemed to make him even angrier.

"My boss thinks it might be a Ukrainian crime family seeking revenge for the murder of one of their guys who was operating a human trafficking ring over in Brooklyn."

"Who? Kos? Yeah, I heard the European trash fuck got knocked off."

"Yeah, apparently his whole crew was taken out a few months back."

Mickey let out a huff. "We noticed things seemed to be quiet over in Brooklyn. That asshole muscled my family out of the prostitution gig about ten years ago. I had a few of my guys discreetly asking around, trying to see whether the crew that took him out was going to step in and claim his territory. I wanted to make sure we weren't dealing with any crazy sick fucks before we moved into Brooklyn and retook what was ours. Get back into the sex business."

Mickey caught himself when he realized that Seth was staring at him with a look of horror on his face.

"Sorry, babe. Sex brings in a lot of money, and I got lots of girls and even a few guys looking to make a bit of extra cash."

"Anyway . . . " Seth shook his head in disgust. "So far, I can't find any evidence to suggest an Eastern European connection to their deaths. All three men worked for you, all three men were lower-level employees, and two out of the three guys seemed to enjoy party drugs."

"What does being a lower-level employee have to do with anything?"

"It just means they were easier to gain access to. Someone like you or your father might be more difficult to locate or get to because you are better at hiding yourselves and your assets. It will take a bit of time, but once I finish looking behind all those shell corporations you're hiding behind . . . I'll find out everything there is to know about you, including where you live."

Mickey let out a chuckle as he leaned back, spreading his legs a bit further apart. "Why are you tryin' to find out where I live? Are you hoping to peek inside and take some dirty pictures of me?" The smirk on Mickey's face was infuriating. The guy clearly had an ego the size of Texas.

"You're an idiot," Seth said, as he took another swig of his beer. He wanted to jump in this guy's lap and feel his hands all over his body, but that smug look on his face infuriated him.

"Either way, tell your boss I got my own man looking into this situation."

"So, you do think these deaths are suspicious." Seth didn't even notice he had shifted closer to Mickey in his excitement.

"My guys are like family. When three of them suddenly become suicidal in a matter of months, I take that shit very seriously. Look, clearly you got some investigative skills. How about you continue looking into this with the help of my guy."

"Who is your guy?"

"Paddy."

The mention of that name sent shivers down Seth's spine. There was no way he was going to work on this investigation with that psychopath. Knowing Patrick, he would take the first opportunity possible to put a bullet in his head, and then claim that Seth accidentally backed up into his flying bullet.

"Ummm, no thanks. I'm not working with your rabid pitbull."

Mickey let out a laugh, then rested a hand on Seth's

thigh. "Paddy is not such a bad guy. Yes, he has some issues. Hell, we all do. But if I ask him to do something, he won't ever betray me. He is loyal to the end."

"How can you be so sure?" Seth asked, eyeing Mickey's hand that was slowly rubbing his thigh.

"Cuz, you're under my protection now. No one from my crew will ever bother you, not even that homophobic dipshit, Brody. Paddy knocked some sense into him because I asked him to. That is the level of loyalty Paddy has for me. We may not be blood-related, but Paddy and I are brothers, and we protect one another."

Mickey's words filled Seth's heart. The loyalty, the comradery, the protection. He had never been so turned on before in his life. He wanted Mickey. He needed Mickey. He wanted Mickey buried deep inside of him, owning every inch of his aching body. It didn't make any sense. But right now, Seth knew only one thing: He wanted Mickey to be his.

Just as Seth was about to pounce on Mickey's rod like a Cougar in heat, Mickey stood up from the couch.

"I'm gonna head. I'll be in touch," Mickey said as he shuffled past Seth on his way to the door.

With disappointment in his eyes, Seth covered his chub and walked Mickey to the door.

Guess his rough boy fuck fantasy was not going to happen after all. Guess it was all just a ploy to get Seth to open up to him.

"Thanks for the ride . . . and for not killing me."

Mickey chuckled. "See ya later, sweet cheeks."

CHAPTER 11- Mickey

It was fucking weird. All night, and again this morning, Mickey's thoughts kept drifting back to Seth. That innocent smile. Those cautious eyes. The way he used sarcasm whenever he was feeling uncomfortable or angry. God, even the way he looked bent over getting railed.

Fuck. He wanted to lay into him. Own him. Protect him. Make him his. His feisty little tiger. Vulnerable, yet venomous.

Normally, Mickey didn't give two shits about people. He fucked them, then moved on with his life. But there was something about Seth that was different. He didn't just want to pound him, then leave. There was something . . .

Last night had been fucked. Mickey had been seconds away from throwing Seth down on the floor and ramming his dick inside him. He knew Seth wanted it. He could see the desire burning in Seth's eyes. But for some strange reason, he didn't want to fuck him against the rough floor and treat him like every other cheap hook-up he'd ever had.

Seth deserved better. There was something in those painful eyes that made Mickey want to protect him. Keep him safe from all the hurt in the world. Give him pleasure like he'd never felt before.

If any of the guys could hear his thoughts . . . fuck—what was wrong with him?

Mickey wanted to know Seth. Ask him questions about his life. Find out what was under that tough, yet vulnerable façade he presented to the world.

That was why Mickey had made the hardest decision of his life and quickly left Seth's apartment. Okay, perhaps he was exaggerating, but once his cock was interested, it was hard to deny the little bugger what it wanted.

Mickey knew if he stayed just a moment longer, Seth would have been staring up at the ceiling, seeing stars, and he would have felt like an asshole.

Now, here he was, stopping by Jaden's shitty apartment, too early in the morning, to have a few words about this guy's ability to do math.

The two-bit hustler had been dodging Mickey all week. Apparently, Jaden got wind that Mickey was stopping by to have a quick chat, and suddenly the man was nowhere to be found.

Hunting his employees down was not one of Mickey's favorite pastimes. Patrick had offered to snatch him up, but

Mickey thought it best to handle this one on his own.

An example needed to be set, and it was always good to remind the crew what happened when you play outside of your square and your deposits were a bit light.

Mickey jumped up onto the fire escape and climbed toward Jaden's fifth-floor apartment. When he reached the bedroom window, he pulled out his switchblade and pried open the window. These old buildings were not designed to keep people out, so he had no issues getting in.

The window slid effortlessly, not making a sound. Inside the bedroom, Jaden lay passed out on the bed, bare white ass exposed for the world to see.

Mickey climbed into his apartment and grabbed the wooden bat that rested next to the bedpost. Now came the fun part.

He stood next to the bed, smiling as he raised the bat and brought it down swiftly against Jaden's bare ass.

The man let out a holler as his body jerked upward. He cupped his ass cheek and squirmed on the bed.

"Mornin' sunshine! You've been dodging my calls."

"Shit!" Jaden cried out, startled, losing his balance, and falling out of bed.

"It's time you and I had a bit of a chat. It seems that either you don't know how to do simple math, or you've been ripping me off. Now, which one is it?" Mickey asked, dropping the bat and grabbing Jaden by the arm.

"Please, boss, I'm sorry."

"You will be."

Mickey spent the next fifteen minutes reminding Jaden how business was done. When he finally left the apartment, Jaden had a busted face, bruised ribs, and a broken lamp.

As he stepped into his car, his stomach grumbled, reminding him that teaching lessons always made him hungry. It was time to grab some food.

Then a thought occurred to him.

CHAPTER 12 – Seth

The buzzer in Seth's apartment rang over and over until Seth finally pressed the *Speak* button.

"What?" Seth yelled into the speaker, annoyed as shit that someone had been so persistent this early in the morning.

"You have a delivery," a muffled voice spoke through the ratty intercom.

"Okay, come on up." Seth pressed the *Unlock* button and listened to the buzzer go off releasing the lock to the main door.

He hadn't ordered anything, so he had no idea what was being delivered. Perhaps it was something from Marc, but Marc would normally let him know something was on its way.

"Sorry, sir. You have to come down to accept this

package. It's too big for one man to handle."

"What? Are you kidding me?" frustration and anger laced his words. Why wouldn't they have brought another guy if the item was too large for one person to carry?

Three minutes later, Seth popped open the front door of his building ready to blast whatever delivery guy couldn't carry a damn package up to his apartment. Instead, his breathing caught in his chest.

"Morning, sweet cheeks."

Mickey grinned, holding out a bag of croissants and a tray of coffee.

"What the . . . ?" Seth's look of frustration was quickly replaced with one of confusion.

"Thought I'd bring over some breakfast. It's a nice day, so I thought we could go 'n eat in the park down the street." Mickey nodded his head toward the green space at the end of the block.

"You mean the park filled with needles and used condoms?" Seth twisted his eyebrows upward looking at the man like he was crazy.

"Well, we can try and find a condom-free bench and hopefully stay away from any needles. Come." Mickey grabbed Seth's hand and pulled him out of the building.

"Why are you here?" Seth asked, glancing at Mickey as he shoved his keys in his jeans.

Seth was grateful that he'd had trouble sleeping last

night, so had gotten up early, showered, and was ready to head out to do some grocery shopping when Mickey happened to drop by. He didn't think he could handle another embarrassing visit by Mickey to his apartment.

"I told you, I brought you breakfast."

"Yeah, but why?"

Mickey glanced at Seth from the corner of his eye, as if contemplating how to respond. After a few minutes, he said, "I figured if you're going to be working with my crew, I should probably get to know you first. Make sure you're not one of them psycho serial killers who drags people back to their cabin an' keeps them under his floorboards."

Seth let out a snort. "This coming from the guy with a kill room in the basement of his strip club."

Mickey smirked. "See, we're getting to know each other already."

"Do I need to let a friend know where I am? If you're planning on killing me, I would like someone to be able to find my body before the animals get to it. I'm too pretty to get my face eaten off."

Seth felt a hand rest on his lower back. "This way."

They walked into the park at the end of the street and came to a halt. Mickey surveyed the area. Garbage, empty beer bottles, open condom wrappers, and other such nightmares littered the park.

"Perhaps you were right about the park. If we sit on any of these benches, we'll need a tetanus shot."

"Or have to check ourselves into the Betty Ford Clinic," Seth added for good measure. "Hey, is that blood on your shirt?" Seth asked, concerned Mickey had somehow gotten jabbed by a stray needle or something.

"Hmm? Oh. No. Well, yes. It is blood, but it's not mine." Mickey held out his shirt noticing the blood for the first time.

Seth stared at him confused. "What? Okay, explain." In what world did you have to ask someone to explain why they had someone else's blood on their shirt?

"It's simple really. I had to teach a guy how to count. Then I came here and brought you croissants." Mickey smiled like that explained everything.

It was probably safer if Seth didn't ask any follow-up questions. Ignorance was bliss and all that jazz . . .

Mickey looked around as if trying to decide what his next move was going to be. "Hmmm. Okay, we eat as we walk. Come."

"Where are we going?" Seth asked.

Mickey grabbed him by the hand and began pulling him down another road. "It's a surprise."

"I'm activating the Find My Friend feature on my phone just in case."

Seth heard Mickey snort as he pulled a croissant out of the bag and handed him one. Somehow, the damn thing was still warm.

They continued to walk another twenty minutes before they came to a street filled with dozens of street vendors and merchants.

Seth's mouth fell open. "Wow, I had no idea there was a vendor's market here." Seth tossed Mickey the bag holding the last croissant and darted toward one of the vendors selling jewelry and apparel made of leather.

"It's all handmade by myself and my daughter," a woman with orange-red hair proudly confessed from behind the table.

"Wow, this stuff is beautiful." Seth picked up a leather bracelet with intricate weaving and designs running along the band. How did he not know this place existed?

"Hi Mickey," the woman greeted, leaning over the table to give the man a hug.

"You know each other?" Seth asked, pointing between the two.

"Oh, yes. I used to babysit Mickey when he was a wee lad. Now, he's all grown up." She leaned forward and pretended to mess up his hair.

"None of that, now." Mickey smiled, as he leaned away from her grasp.

He couldn't help but smile at the playful interaction between the woman and Mickey. Perhaps Mickey was not the brutish gangster the media would have you believe. The joyful smile and beaming white teeth made Seth's heart swoon.

Remembering that he was broke, Seth placed the bracelet down on the table and thanked the lady for her help. The woman simply nodded as Seth walked toward the next booth to continue his 'window shopping.'

"Oh, wow! Mickey! Come check this out!"

Mickey materialized beside Seth and was suddenly assaulted by a green and black scarf with shamrocks stitched throughout the material. The material was thin and delicate, something more suited to Seth's fashion sense than Mickey's.

"Hmmm. I think it looked better in my mind than on you." Seth scrunched his face then pulled the scarf off disappointed. "Let's keep looking."

As they moved from one booth to the next, Seth took the opportunity to get to know this mysterious hunk of man. It turned out that Mickey was a Taurus, born at the beginning of May, which made him organized, stubborn, fiercely loyal, perfect for leadership roles, and a hopeless romantic. Mickey scoffed his nose at this last one. Seth, on the other hand, was a Virgo, being logical, practical, kind, gentle, and always wanting to help others.

Mickey didn't put too much stock into astrological signs. "It's all a bunch of horseshit. No moon or water god is going to tell me who I can and cannot stick my dick into."

"God, you're romantic," Seth replied, sarcasm oozing from his words.

"Just sayin'. We decide our own lives. If you don't like something, change it."

"I just find it kind of romantic to think that you are predestined to be with someone. That the Universe has selected that one special someone who was created just for you." Seth's mind drifted off as he hoped to one day find that special someone, made for just him.

"There's nothing wrong with that . . . " Mickey's voice trailed off as he spotted an elderly woman struggling with some grocery bags. "One sec."

Mickey darted across the street and began conversing with the elderly woman, who was joined by a little boy. Seth walked up to the group and smiled.

"Seth, this is Mrs. McCarthy and her grandson, Ben." Mickey pulled grocery bags from the woman's hands.

"It's nice to meet you, ma'am," Seth greeted as he took some of the woman's bags as well.

"Where are you parked, Mrs. McCarthy?" Mickey asked, looking around the street for her car.

"Oh, I stopped driving that thing two years ago. Marty was the one who always drove us around."

Mickey gave Seth a pleading look. "It's okay, Seth and I will help you carry these bags back to your house."

"You don't have to do that, sweety. Ben and I can manage just fine."

The woman was 5'2 with a fragile frame. The only thing she was handling was making sure her dentures didn't fall out of her mouth as she spoke.

When they arrived at Mrs. McCarthy's house, Seth entertained Ben in the backyard while Mickey helped put away the groceries. Once the fridge was loaded and cupboards stocked, Mrs. McCarthy came out into the backyard carrying some cold sodas and homemade biscuits.

"I want some!" Ben squealed as he came running across the yard and jumped into one of the deck chairs.

The woman had a selection of mismatched deck chairs that appeared to have been collected over the years. They came in all different colors and sizes.

Seth thanked Mrs. McCarthy when she handed him a drink and watched Mickey disappear around the side of the house. A few minutes later, he reappeared shirtless hauling a lawnmower.

"Oh, don't worry about that! I'll cut the grass tomorrow!" the woman yelled across the lawn.

Mickey held his hand up to his ear pretending that he couldn't hear her.

"That boy is one of the good ones."

Seth turned to face Mrs. McCarthy, who was watching Mickey start the lawnmower and then begin cutting her grass. It was clear that Mickey seemed to care a lot about the people in his community, from the vendors they visited today to Mrs. McCarthy and her grandson. This was a quality Seth admired.

"He always makes sure everyone is taken care of in the community."

"Have you known Mickey a long time?"

"I've known the O'Briens since Mickey's father was just a boy. I even dated his granddaddy for a few months back in the day."

"So, you must know Mickey pretty well then." Seth reached for a biscuit and took a bite.

"You look like a smart young man, so I won't insult your intelligence by lying to you. I'm sure you know what Mickey's family does for a living?"

Seth nodded.

"What you need to understand is that his family takes care of the community. Clive, Mickey's father, conducts business with an old-world mentality; men take care of women, and women should never question their husbands. Mickey, on the other hand, runs his business from the heart. He sees everyone as family and does what's best for the collective as a whole. Clive would never have come over and cut my lawn. He would have sent one of his goons to come and do it. That is the type of person Mickey is. He cares for people and doesn't see himself as next in line to run the O'Brien family."

Seth turned his focus back to Mickey, who was working up quite a sweat in the late afternoon heat.

"He really is something else," Seth whispered to himself.

"Yes, dear, he is. I hope one day he will find a partner who will stand with him and inspire him to be the great leader we all need him to be. Jersey is going to hell quickly. We need people like Mickey to keep us safe." The woman placed her hand on Seth's and gave it a little pat.

It wasn't lost on Seth that the woman said "partner" instead of wife. Seth wondered what other secrets this woman might be keeping. Having lived all these years in the same community, she was bound to be a wealth of information.

"I'll be back in a moment." Seth picked up one of the chilled sodas and brought it down to Mickey who looked hot and thirsty.

Mickey's face lit up as Seth brought him the drink.

"Thought you could use a drink."

"Thanks, sweet cheeks." Mickey winked at Seth as he gulped down the soda.

Seth watched as a bead of sweat slid down Mickey's chiseled chest and abs. It took every ounce of his strength not to jump Mickey right there on Mrs. McCarthy's lawn. The man was a fucking beast. Knowing the man was hot as well as kind, made Seth want him even more.

CHAPTER 13 - Seth

On the way back to Seth's apartment, Mickey insisted on picking up some takeout from a little Italian restaurant a block from his apartment. They ordered risotto, chicken parmigiana, and bruschetta.

The food smelled amazing as Seth carried empty plates into the living room of his tiny apartment. "Sorry again for the lack of space. Good thing you're not claustrophobic."

Seth went back into the kitchen to grab some beers while Mickey filled their plates.

Mickey chuckled. "It's fine. Sit down and join me." He cleared off the couch cushion and passed Seth a plate with some risotto and chicken on it. "The food at this place is amazing. You're going to love it."

Seth watched as Mickey shoved a fork full of rice into his gorgeous mouth. How was it possible for someone to look this sexy in horrible lighting?

"Here, try this." Mickey picked up a piece of chicken with his fork and brought it to Seth's mouth. For a moment, they stared into each other's eyes, not moving. Time stood still as each was drawn toward the other.

Heart pounding, Seth broke eye contact, leaned forward, and bit down on the chicken. There was an explosion of flavor as Seth's tastebuds came to life.

A deep moan escaped his lips as he allowed the flavors to consume his body. "Wow, that is amazing!" Seth declared, rushing to shovel another forkful of food into his mouth.

"Yes. Amazing," Mickey replied, licking some sauce off his lower lip as he stared at Seth.

Why did Seth get the feeling Mickey wasn't talking about the food? He began nervously eating, trying not to stare at the sexy Irish stud sitting next to him.

Once they finished dinner, Mickey cleared the plates while Seth placed the leftovers in the fridge. It was kind of nice having someone else in his space. It felt very domestic cleaning up after dinner together as if they were a real couple. Only in his wildest dreams.

Back on the couch, Seth sat with one leg under his butt, facing the tattooed beefcake currently taking up three-quarters of his couch.

"I have to ask—how tall are you, man?" Seth asked, admiring how gorgeous Mickey's green eyes looked in the soft moonlight.

Mickey looked up toward the ceiling as if searching for the answers. "I think six-foot one? Been a while since I measured."

Why did everything coming out of this man's mouth sound so dirty . . . and so sexual?

"What are you? Five-foot seven?"

Seth placed his hand to his heart feigning offense. "I'm five-foot eight!"

"I was close." Mickey smirked.

"Hey! Every inch counts!"

"Especially when trying to hit that G-spot," Mickey joked, giving Seth a wicked grin.

He couldn't take it anymore. Without thinking, Seth lunged into Mickey's lap, straddling his legs. He brought his hungry lips savagely to Mickey's, kissing him hard and deep.

To Seth's surprise, Mickey grabbed the back of his head and pushed his lips even harder against Seth's. Mickey's tongue slowly invaded Seth's mouth, massaging his tongue, as his lips desperately wrestled against Seth's.

Seth felt Mickey's powerful arm wrap itself around his body and pull him tight against his chest. The hunger and desperation were like nothing he had ever felt before. They couldn't get close enough.

He couldn't believe this was happening. Talk about his hottest fantasy come true.

This smoking hot, badass, mother fucker was making out with him. Claiming him. Making him his own personal play toy.

At least for tonight, anyway.

Who cared? If tonight was all he got, so be it. Tonight's sexcapades would live on in his memory and jerk off fantasies for the rest of his life.

Right now, he just wanted this hot Irish beefcake inside him. Claiming him. Pounding into him.

Seth moaned as he felt Mickey's cock harden between his legs. It was such a turn-on knowing he was the one turning on this ripped delicious badass. *He* was the one making Mickey's dick hard. Fuck.

As if sensing Seth's desperation, Mickey wrapped his powerful arms under Seth's firm ass and lifted him off the couch.

Seth wrapped his legs around Mickey's waist, marveling at the strength of this sex god, while Mickey carried him into his bedroom.

Mickey gently placed Seth on the bed and yanked Seth's shirt off his body in one swift and violent motion.

Seth let out a squeak as his shirt was ripped from his body. Secretly, Seth enjoyed being manhandled in the bedroom. Having a guy take control and go all caveman on his ass was such a turn-on.

Mickey pulled off his own shirt and tossed it over his shoulders. With heated eyes, Mickey lowered his hard body between Seth's spread thighs.

"Fuck—you're gorgeous," Mickey whispered. His hand gently caressed Seth's face as he searched longingly into the depths of his golden-brown eyes.

Seth had never felt so wanted. So desired. Was this really happening?

"Please. I'm nothing compared to you. You're the smoking hot stud everyone wants. I can't believe you are actually turned on by someone like me," Seth confessed, lowering his eyes bashfully and focusing on Mickey's lips instead. He knew he was cute, but he never thought of himself as gorgeous.

"That's where you're wrong. I've wanted you since the moment I saw you sitting at that bar. You have the courage to stand up for yourself, even against thugs like Brody. You have such kind and gentle eyes." Mickey continued to caress Seth's face. "Your lips are sinfully delicious, and you're humble enough not to realize just how fucking sexy you really are. Plus, you have a smoking hot body I can't fuckin' wait to bury my cock into."

Seth felt his cheeks flush at the sweet words coming from Mickey. Did he really see him that way? Seth wanted him even more now.

"Yes, please get to the burying your cock deep inside me part!" Seth exclaimed with the excitement of a child waking up on Christmas morning. He could not wait to be stretched out and start seeing stars.

Mickey chuckled at Seth's excitement and began

kissing every inch of his body.

Seth struggled to contain himself when Mickey kissed his neck, then slowly moved his mouth downward, exploring every inch of Seth's body. The attention he gave to each new body part had Seth quivering. Mickey was not having sex with Seth; Mickey was worshiping his body.

"God, you feel amazing," Seth moaned as he enjoyed the sensation of Mickey's rough lips on his smooth body. He gripped the bedspread as he convulsed once more against Mickey's sensual touch.

When Mickey finally reached Seth's waistband, he looked up and gave him a devilish grin. The hungry look of those emerald eyes looking up at him almost made him come in his pants.

"You've got such amazing eyes." Seth couldn't help but be mesmerized by the vivid green. They seemed to call to him, summoning him to let go and give in to his greatest desires. Give in to the powerful beast currently claiming his body.

"I got my emerald eyes from my Irish roots, but my devilish tongue from my French roots." Mickey gave him another one of his evil smiles, driving Seth mad.

He unbuttoned Seth's jeans and pulled them off with a feral groan.

Seth's eyes narrowed as he watched Mickey step off the bed.

"Take it easy, little bird. Just giving you a show as I

remove these," Mickey whispered, eyes locked on Seth's as he popped open the top button on his jeans.

Slowly, Mickey unzipped, watching Seth as he licked his lower lip. With heated eyes, Seth watched as Mickey pulled down his jeans and boxer briefs in one teasing swoop. Seth let out a gasp as Mickey's thick cock bounced up against his abdomen. Fuck—that was hot.

Mickey smirked.

"Yes please, Daddy." Seth groaned, eyes fixated on the hard piece of meat between Mickey's thighs.

"Hey, you're only seven years younger than me. I'm too young to be your daddy," Mickey argued, mock offended by the comment.

"When the other guy is twice your size, you become *his* bitch in bed. And I hate to tell you, but those arms of yours are twice the size of my legs. So, I *am* . . . at *your* mercy . . . Daddy!" This time, Seth gave Mickey a devilish smirk.

Mickey growled as he climbed back on the bed, positioning himself between Seth's legs. He licked the tip of Seth's cock, teasing him before he placed his mouth over the head and swallowed the full length of his shaft.

Seth let out a groan, throwing his head back in ecstasy. Watching his cock disappear into Mickey's hot mouth was sinfully delicious. He wanted to engrave this image into his mind permanently.

The suction around his cock intensified to the point Seth was certain he was about to blow his load right there in Mickey's mouth. Just when he couldn't take it any longer, Mickey's strong arms wrapped around his thin body, suddenly flipping him onto his stomach with no effort at all.

The cool air hitting Seth's bare ass made his cheeks clench.

"Now that is a delicious ass," Mickey growled before burying his face between Seth's cheeks without warning.

"Oh, God!" Seth shouted as his ass was invaded by Satan's mouth and tongue. He was in heaven. It was both aggressive and tender at the same time.

Mickey played off every moan and spasm of Seth's body. Teasing him. Playing with him. Ensuring Seth felt every pleasure and intense sensation possible. The guy was a fucking god in bed.

After having his ass eaten for what felt like an eternity, Seth heard the sound of a condom being ripped open. He glanced over his shoulder and watched as Mickey rolled the condom down the full length of his shaft.

Next, he opened a tiny bottle he pulled out of god knows where, and began lubing up his impressive cock.

Seth couldn't wait to feel Mickey deep inside him. He had fantasized about this moment ever since they first met. Well . . . after he realized that the man was not about to murder him.

"Are you ready, sweet cheeks?"

Seth nodded as he felt Mickey press the head of his

cock between his soft cheeks. The anticipation was exhilarating. Knowing that at any moment, Mickey's cock would be spreading his ass cheeks open.

Seth took a deep breath as Mickey slowly pushed his dick inside him and past that first ring of muscle. He could feel every inch as it slid deeper and deeper, stretching him open inch by inch.

Just when he thought he couldn't take another inch, Mickey stopped moving.

"Does that hurt? Are you okay?" his voice was soft and gentle. Seth could hear the genuine concern in his voice.

Most tops just worried about jamming their dick inside and didn't care how painful it was for the bottom. Seth was a little caught off guard by the level of concern in Mickey's voice. He seemed to genuinely care about Seth's well-being.

Judging by his movements, Mickey appeared to be holding back. Was he afraid of hurting him?

For that, he wanted Mickey even more. He needed him. He wanted to be claimed by him.

"Yes, you feel amazing," Seth whispered as he tilted his head back pressing his soft lips against Mickey's hungry mouth.

Mickey began rolling his hips, forcing his cock in and out of Seth's tight hole.

"More. I want more. I want you to pound me hard," Seth's voice sounded needy and desperate. He wanted to be

Mickey's. He needed to be owned. "Fuck me, hard, baby."

With Seth's permission, he stopped holding back. He tightened his grip around Seth's narrow hips and began thrusting his cock into Seth's tight hole, deep and without mercy.

Seth let out a squeal as his ass was impaled by Mickey's thick cock. He felt so full and sore at the same time but secretly loved the feeling. With each pump, he felt more and more connected to Mickey.

Each thrust seemed to brush up against Seth's prostate sending waves of pleasure throughout his body.

Just when he thought he couldn't take any more of Mickey's cock, Mickey wrapped his arms around Seth and pulled him firmly against his body.

Seth was now seated on Mickey's lap as he thrust upward into his guts. He could feel his balls tighten and suddenly all he could see were stars.

Without even touching his cock, Seth let out a moan as he shot his load all over his bedspread. This was apparently all Mickey needed to lose his mind.

He immediately started pounding hard into Seth, ignoring Seth's sudden gasps of pain, until he too let out a powerful growl and began shooting his load deep inside Seth's tight ass.

Exhausted, they both fell forward on the bed. Seth landed in his own cum while Mickey's large body flopped overtop of his tiny frame. Seth let out a huff as the weight of Mickey's body crashed down on him.

Mickey chuckled and pulled Seth's helpless body out from beneath him. "Hope I didn't crush you, sweet cheeks."

Seth curled his sweaty body into Mickey's solid frame. He could barely catch his breath. No one had ever fucked him so hard before. He knew he would be feeling that one for days.

"I'm happy to be crushed by your heavy body any day, as long as you're naked and on top of me." Seth nuzzled his head into the crook of Mickey's arm and breathed in his masculine scent. God, he smelled like sweat and cum. So hot.

Mickey let out a chuckle and squeezed Seth tight against his body. "I'm happy to crush you anytime as long as you're naked as well, sexy." He leaned forward and kissed the top of Seth's head.

This simple tender act filled Seth's heart with joy. This was where he wanted to be; held tightly in Mickey's strong arms.

He felt safe and secure like he was the only person who mattered to Mickey.

The light from the moon draped over their naked bodies in a perfect silhouette. Wrapped in each other's embrace, sleep eventually overtook them.

CHAPTER 14- Mickey

Light from the moon drifted in through the window and kissed the boy's face as he slept. Seth's delicate features seemed almost Angelic resting under the evening's midnight glow. How could someone so beautiful exist in such a violent and ugly world?

He looked so gentle and peaceful like he didn't have a care in the world. It was during these times when the mind relaxed and drifted off into a carefree world that people were truly the happiest. In the dream world, anything was possible; there were no limits and endless possibilities. How could one not be happy?

Mickey lay on his side, watching his beautiful little tiger sleep. He couldn't help but wonder how this gentle creature before him had ended up taming his wild heart.

Over the years, Mickey had hundreds of sexual partners, both male and female, but none of them ever made him feel the peace and euphoria he currently felt.

There was something about this boy. Something about this timid little bunny who was masquerading around in the stripes of a tiger. Yes, Seth put on a tough exterior when confronted, but deep down, he was just a terrified young man looking for someone to protect him from all the evils of the world.

Mickey wanted to be that protector.

Gently, he brushed a few strands of stray hairs from Seth's forehead. He looked so peaceful.

As he stared longingly at his sleeping beauty, he wondered, was it even possible for someone so sweet to ever fall in love with someone so dangerous? More accurately put, could an angel ever fall in love with a demon?

Mickey feared that once Seth got to know him and discovered who he really was, there was no way he would ever want to be with him. Mickey was a monster, who tried to cover up his evil acts with good deeds. But who was he kidding?

No one could ever love a monster like him.

With that disheartening thought, Mickey gently crept out of Seth's bed, doing his best not to disturb his sleeping angel.

Gently, he crept across the linoleum flooring searching for his clothing.

After a moment, he managed to locate his underwear

which had been tossed against the wall during their hurried frenzy to get naked. He pulled them on and made his way into the tiny living room.

He didn't bother turning on a lamp; there was enough light streaming in through the windows that Mickey had no issues seeing in the dark.

He stood in the center of the room and glanced around the apartment. The apartment was small with only one bedroom. It was located in one of the rougher neighborhoods in Jersey. The exposed brick and floor radiators added to the rustic feel of the place. Seth had tried to spruce up the place by adding splashes of color throughout the living space, but all it managed to do was make the apartment look less "drug den" and more "starving student."

Mickey walked around, flipping through books and checking out pictures. It didn't take Mickey long to notice that all the photos on display were of Seth and his friends, all taken within the last few years.

There were no pictures of family members or celebrations from years past. It was as if Seth's life started only a few years ago.

He wondered if Seth was estranged from his family. Did they have a falling out? Was he kicked out of his parents' home? Was he an orphan?

These were all answers that Mickey longed to discover. He wanted to get to know Seth. The real Seth. The man behind the smile and sad eyes.

But then again, what was the point?

It's not like they could ever have a future together. He could never be in a relationship with a guy.

Fucking around here and there was one thing but holding hands and announcing to the world that he was in a relationship with a man was something completely different.

If his old man ever found out he would put a bullet in his head and toss his body in the Hudson. No son of his would be a faggot.

His mind drifted back to the terrifying night where he witnessed his father beating his friend's dad because he kissed a man. Imagine what he would do to his son who was fuckin' a man.

O'Brien men weren't gay. Or bisexual. They were hetero men, who loved pussy . . . and that's it.

Mickey adjusted his waistband and walked to the large living room window.

Down below, the streets were quiet. Most people had retired for the night, except for those looking to party.

Mickey counted six hookers on various corners and three drug dealers. He wasn't judging. Hell, that was how he earned eighty percent of his income. There was always money to be made in drugs and sex. People loved to get high, and people loved to fuck.

As he stood at the window watching the world beneath him drift by, his mind drifted to his childhood.

From what he could remember, the first few years of his childhood had been great. His mother was one of those people everyone loved to be around. She organized playdates with all the kids in the neighborhood so all the mothers and kids had a chance to socialize and support one another. She worked with other women to set up collections and donations to help families who had fallen on hard times, and she even hosted a weekly barbeque during the summer for all their friends and neighbors.

But Sofia's true talent was in her storytelling. She loved to create fantasy worlds filled with ogres and wizards and little boys who went on dangerous adventures. In all of her stories, the hero's name was a variation of the name Mickey.

Mickey always imagined himself on those adventures, protecting the villagers from all the beasts and monsters. He was the protector, the hero.

His father, on the other hand, was not impressed with his wife's wild stories. Each time he would scold her for putting such 'pansy' ideas in their son's head.

Mickey resented his father for belittling his mother. Over the years, he watched as the spark slowly faded from his mother's eyes. Her once happy zest for life became morose and sullen.

As Mickey got older, he realized the true cause of his mother's unhappiness was his father. His toxic life and ever-growing distant personality.

Eventually, the unthinkable happened. Mickey's

mother was killed in a car accident. Mickey was only eleven when his mother's car was pulled out of the Passaic River. For months, Mickey retreated into himself, refusing to speak to anyone or even play with the other children.

It wasn't until a nine-year-old by the name of Patrick moved into the neighborhood that he began to speak and play once again.

Both had lost their mothers at a young age; Mickey's had passed away while Patrick's had runoff. Both feared and hated their fathers who were mean-spirited and angry men. So naturally, both boys bonded and became fast friends.

Mickey often wondered if his mother had lived, would his father have become a gentler man? Would Mickey have continued to follow in his father's footsteps?

While his father's crew made the majority of their money through criminal activities, Mickey tried to balance these sins by giving back to the community whenever possible.

Each year, they donated thousands of dollars to various neighborhood charities and children's hospitals, collected food and toys for struggling families in the neighborhood, and even hosted community barbeques twice a month where families in the neighborhood could stop by with their kids and enjoy free food.

Functions like these helped to build a sense of community and keep Mickey aware of activities in the neighborhood.

Some of the guys even ran an afterschool sports camp for local kids in the community. They hoped the camp would keep kids busy and out of trouble while helping single parents who couldn't afford daycare or afterschool activities.

Then last year, "bleeding heart" Dominic, decided it would be a nice idea to offer "late-night escort services" for elderly women. No, not fucking elderly women late at night "services" . . . but walking elderly women (and some men) home or to appointments late at night as a sort of safety and protection detail.

Apparently, Dominic's Nonna had been mugged while on her way to the pharmacy one night, so Dominic decided the neighborhood needed an elderly escort service. So, Dominic and a few other tough-looking crew members began running this service.

As an FYI, don't ever piss off an Italian or mess with his Nonna. Let's just say the mugger was found three days later, dead in a dumpster, missing both his hands. To this day, they are still searching for his hands.

Yes, Mickey's life was a rough and complicated one. Who in their right mind could ever fall in love with such a man?

Mickey inhaled sharply as two soft and cold hands wrapped themselves around his bare stomach.

From the darkness, Seth's gentle features emerged as he stepped into the moonlight.

Mickey interlocked his fingers with Seth's as he turned

to face his sleepy little man.

"What are you doing up?" Seth asked in a groggy voice. Sleep still clung to the boy as he tried to remain upright.

Mickey could feel the weight of Seth's body leaning against his as he continued his losing battle against sleep. "Sorry if I woke you. I couldn't sleep," Mickey whispered as he turned and wrapped his muscular arms around the sleepy young man.

Leaning into his body, it appeared that Mickey's embrace was just the thing Seth needed to win his battle against sleep. His eyes heated and an evil grin materialized.

A moment later, Seth slid down the length of his body, stopping momentarily to reach into Mickey's boxers and pull out his rapidly thickening cock.

Mickey stood in the moonlight, watching Seth as his hungry mouth swallowed the thickness of his shaft all the way down to the base. He couldn't help but moan as Seth opened his throat and forced down every last inch of his delicious meat.

He admired Seth's perfect red lips as they slid up and down his solid shaft. His determined little tiger looked so perfect swallowing his cock.

Using both of his hands, Mickey grabbed the back of Seth's head and forced his cock deeper into his hot, wet mouth. Seth moaned and gagged as he opened himself up to Mickey's manhood.

He smiled knowing this hungry young man was enjoying the taste of his cock. He couldn't contain himself any longer and began pumping into the boy's mouth without mercy.

Tears slid down Seth's face as he sacrificed breathing in order to swallow even more of Mickey's cock.

Mickey finally reached the edge and let out a furious roar, spilling his seed down Seth's eager throat.

His gorgeous angel swallowed every last drop, gazing up at Mickey with adoration.

Seth licked the cum off the corner of his mouth as he gently placed Mickey's cock back in his shorts. The sinful look in Seth's eyes made Mickey's dick twitch once more.

Fuck. This boy was going to be trouble.

CHAPTER 15 - Seth

The following morning, Seth opened his eyes to the sight of Mickey fumbling with his jeans, trying to fasten his button while sticking his head through the top of his shirt. If Seth didn't know better, it looked as though Mickey was trying to sneak out of his apartment without saying goodbye. Typical closet case.

What is it with guys freaking out after having a night of hot and steamy sex? It was like the second a guy came, his vision cleared, and he could suddenly see the errors of his way.

Seth had watched his fair share of blokes stumble and fall as they rushed to get out of his apartment. Was there something wrong with him? Guys seemed to love it when he was sucking their dicks. What changed between then and emptying their balls? Fuck it.

"Sneaking out without even saying goodbye?" Seth

asked, propping his head up on one arm.

Mickey jerked free of his shirt, looking like the cat that ate the canary. "Uh, well . . . I didn't want to wake you. Figured I'd let you sleep while I headed home to change."

Seth noticed that Mickey was having trouble making eye contact.

Yup, another breeder takes a walk on the gay side and then freaks out. Fucker's remorse.

Seth rolled his eyes. He was too tired for this shit. "Sure, thing. Thanks for the fuck last night. See ya around." Seth rolled his body so he was facing the window. He didn't need to see yet another man walk away.

He listened to the sound of Mickey's footsteps crossing the linoleum flooring. They stopped when he reached his bedroom door. Seth refused to turn around.

"Ummm . . . I should probably get your number. Just in case you find out anything useful about the case," Mickey's voice was soft and unsure.

Like he was ever going to share information with this asshole. "Yeah, sure." Seth spit out his cell phone number and listened to Mickey as he said "bye" and closed the front door behind him.

Fuck him. While the familiar sting of rejection stabbed at him, he secretly hoped Mickey would call.

Fat chance of that. As Seth predicted, the rest of the week went by without a word from Mickey. He was just another one-night stand, same as all the other big-dicked jerks he slept with. Why was he always chasing after the wrong men?

They all claimed to have enjoyed themselves, yet after they were done using his body, they all disappeared.

Why was he hoping Mickey would be any different?

Seth kept himself busy during the week by attending classes, reviewing surveillance footage from the crime scenes, and dealing with last-minute details for Eve's Night of Debauchery and Sin this Saturday night.

The bachelorette party started with pre-drinks at Seth's place which included a signature cocktail Seth liked to call, Eve's Passion—a combination of pineapple, white wine, ginger ale, and white grapes.

As the glasses emptied, people shared their favorite Eve moments, including a hilarious story involving a dominatrix outfit, a nun, and a talking parrot. Somewhere, out there, was a traumatized parrot and a confused nun.

Seth was surprised when Alex and Marc showed up at his door. He had hoped they would attend, but with Marc's antisocial personality, it was hit or miss as to whether they would actually show up.

By the time they made it to Le Grand Papa, Seth had a nice buzz going. It had been ages since Seth let himself party hard, so tonight his goal was to get "white girl wasted." Tonight, was all about partying hard with Eve and her fellow gay boys and girls.

Seth had arranged reserved seating right next to the

stage so Eve could be pulled up on stage when her favorite drag queen, Lady Mystical, came out to perform.

Eve's face lit up when Lady Mystical arrived on stage dressed as Lady Gaga in one of her outfits from her Monster Ball Tour.

She threw back the remainder of her pink drink, waving her arms frantically to get the attention of her idol. She didn't have to work hard. Within seconds, Eve was being pulled on stage and given a mic.

Eve let out a screech as she wrapped her arms around her new best friend and the two belted out show tunes.

Word of advice: never sit in the front row when a drunk Eve is performing on stage. You're likely to end up catching a face full of pink martini or an eye full of red panties.

At 11:30 it was time to hit the strip club. The band of horny gays shook their sexy little asses as they entered the Den of Sin and Mayhem.

The haunting lyrics of *Alive*, sung by Drain's all female rocker group welcomed the boys to heaven on earth. A magical place where all your fantasies could come true . . . for a price.

The crowd cheered as two men wearing only football gear took turns grinding up against a blond boy's bent-over ass. Apparently, the young athlete had lost a contact and the other guys were helping him find it on stage. This was the true definition of "working as a team."

Oh, look. Now the jock decided to confess all his sins to the team captain who's joined them on stage.

The group followed Eve as she skipped her way through the club, finding the perfect set of tables located in Pervert's Row.

Pervert's Row—the row located right next to the stage—was also commonly known as the "splash zone." You never quite knew what bodily fluid might end up hitting you in the eye or landing in your drink. Viewers beware.

Marc pulled out a chair at the end of the table and wiped . . . something . . . off the seat before sitting down. He gave Alex a disgusted look, then pulled Alex into his lap. Alex made himself comfortable and smiled when he felt something beneath him begin to thicken.

"Mmmm, that better be because of me and not because of 'Mr. All Muscles and No Brains' up there." Alex nodded toward the bent-over "receiver" as he pulled out a small bottle of hand sanitizer and squirted some into Marc's left hand. You couldn't be too careful when it came to touching surfaces . . . Especially in the "squirt zone."

"It's all you, babe. My dick is allergic to your ass. It always swells up when they touch." Alex burst out laughing at Marc's attempt at a joke.

"God, I love you, babe." Alex leaned in and kissed his fiancé.

Seth grinned as he watched this loving exchange between his friends. He couldn't wait until he found his own special someone. Someone to share inside jokes with and loving stares.

"Okay, so what is one thing you're looking forward to when you get married? And what's one thing that scares you?" Seth asked as he passed Eve the tray of shots that had just been delivered to their table.

"You waited until this girl was wasted out of her mind to ask her such deep questions?" Eve yelled as she downed a shot. Her eyes squeezed shut as she sucked on a lime. "Damn—that was good!"

"You had to be! This way we are guaranteed to get a truthful answer," Alex joked as he leaned in and placed his hand on her shoulder.

Eve placed her hand over his, seeming to enjoy the feeling of being connected with her friends. When Eve had transitioned from Evan to Eve, she'd lost a lot of friends who didn't understand or were unwilling to be supportive of her journey. She was grateful to have met such a great set of friends who had quickly become her chosen family.

"Well, I'm looking forward to waking up next to James' smiling face every morning. Knowing that no matter how hard things get, he will always be there by my side, supporting me and holding my hand."

A sea of groans erupted from the heavily intoxicated group.

"God, that's sweet." Seth picked up his cocktail and chugged it.

"Don't worry, *baby gay*. One day you will find yourself a hunky slab of beef who will spend his morning creep watching you while you sleep." Eve patted the side of Seth's cheek.

Alex burst out laughing and turned to face Marc. Apparently, Alex and Marc had their own set of inside jokes going.

"Let's hope." Seth raised his glass toward Eve.

"And what are you terrified of?" Marc asked, peering over Alex's shoulder while still holding him tight around the waist.

Eve scrunched her face as she thought long and hard. "I guess if I had to choose . . . Dutch ovens."

The group went silent, wondering what on earth she was talking about.

"I swear, if I'm ever under the covers sucking his dick and he lets one rip, I'm going to bite his fucking dick off. Then, that will be the end of my marriage. There is no way I'm staying married to a dickless man." She picked up her blueberry cocktail and took a sip as though she were discussing the weather.

The group burst out laughing while some pretended to gag.

A few minutes later, a sea of rock-hard cocks advanced on the group. Everywhere Seth turned, he was assaulted by meat. Thank God he wasn't a vegetarian . . . or straight.

Marty pulled out a twenty and watched as two dancers

battled for access to his zipper. Each one trying to land their ass on the goal post between his legs. Eventually, the dark-haired jock won and the red-haired twink dragged his losing feet toward another table.

Seth felt sorry for the poor brown-haired jock who made the mistake of approaching Marc and Alex. He literally jumped in the air when Marc let out a growl.

"No problem, bud. Not interested. I get it," the terrified jock blurted before stepping back and away from danger.

Seth had never seen a stripper back away so cautiously before. It was like watching a deer back away from a lion. One wrong move and the beast was likely to pounce.

Hating himself, he glanced at his phone for the hundredth time that evening. Nothing.

Was he really expecting to find anything different? Why was he torturing himself? The guy was straight. He had an itch. Seth scratched it. He should be happy that he got to ride on such an incredible dick.

Bottom line: He wasn't interested.

"So, who are you waiting to hear from?" Eve lowered her voice as she leaned forward.

"Hmm? Oh, no one. Nothing." Seth flipped his phone downward and took another shot of tequila. Who's idea was it to get tequila?

"Doesn't seem like nothing," Eve prodded.

Seth glanced at the rest of the group, all currently

distracted, talking amongst themselves or busy rubbing dollar bills across washboard abs.

"Honestly, it's just a hook-up I had earlier in the week. At the time, it felt like we had a real connection. He kept telling me how hot I was, staring into my eyes. I really thought there might be something there."

"And I'm guessing you haven't heard from him since?"

It was the ever-repeating tragedy of single gay men everywhere.

Seth nodded his head. He felt hurt and angry. Hurt at being rejected, and angry at being played.

"Just try and be patient, sweety. The right man is out there wondering the exact same thing as you. One day you'll both find each other and it will be me holding you down while that hunk of beef over there cock slaps your face."

Seth laughed. Eve always knew how to make him feel better. That was one of the things that drew Seth to Eve, her constant positivity and charisma. "Thanks, babe."

Two hours later, Seth nearly jumped out of his skin when his cell phone buzzed in his pocket, pulling him out of his drunken stupor.

He stared at the phone but the numbers on the display were all jumbled.

How had he gotten so drunk?

However it had happened, he was fuckin' loving it.

"Hello?" Seth shouted into the phone. He could barely hear the voice on the other end. "Speak up, dude! I can't hear shit!" he shouted into the receiver. "Hello?" he tried again, but still could not hear over the blaring music and loud whistles. "Hold on one sec."

Seth stumbled out of his chair and made his way to a quieter section of the bar.

"Hello?" Seth asked once again, wondering what time it was, and why his mouth felt so dry.

"Seth?" a male voice asked.

"Yeah, who is this?"

"It's Mickey."

Seth almost dropped the phone in shock. He shook his head and composed himself before bringing the phone back to his ear. "Oh, hey. What's it going on?" his words were jumbled. He was trying his best to sound cool and relaxed, even though his mind and heart were racing a mile a minute.

"Where are you? What's all that noise?" Mickey asked.

"I'm out. What do you want, Mickey?" his voice was a little more aggressive than he intended, but he was drunk and still a little hurt, so fuck him.

"Out where? Are you drunk?"

"Yes, I'm shit-faced!" he shouted into the phone, staring up at the ceiling. "What the fuck do you want, Mr. Irish Man?"

"Seth, where the fuck are you? And who are you out with?" Mickey growled through the phone.

His aggressive tone caught Seth off guard and made him flinch.

"I'm at Eve's bachelorette party watching some dudes fuck on stage. What's it any of your business?"

"What? Dudes fucking? Where are you? I'm coming to get you!"

Seth laughed into the phone. "Seriously, dude. Go fuck yourself." He hung up and jammed his phone into his pocket.

Immediately, he felt his phone vibrating against his leg.

Who does this dick think he is? *"Where are you?" "I'm coming to get you."* Please. I'm having a great fucking time with my besties.

Seth got back to the table and downed two more shots. It was probably not the smartest idea, but who the fuck cared? He had nowhere to be and no one to answer to.

It was just after 4 AM when Seth stumbled out of the cab, catching himself just before falling on the concrete. He waved to Eve and Marty as their cab sped off into the darkness.

"Catch you later, bitches!" Seth called out as the lights of the cab disappeared in the distance.

He shoved his hand into his pocket and fished for his keys. They were in there somewhere . . .

"About fucking time," an angry voice growled from behind.

Seth let out a yelp as he spun around, startled.

Mickey grabbed Seth by the wrist, squeezing hard enough to make him wince. "Where the fuck were you all night? And why are you so fuckin' drunk?"

Seth yanked his arm free from Mickey's grasp and glared at Mickey. "Why's it any of your fucking business where I was and how much I drank? What the hell are you even doing here?"

"I've been waiting for you to come home," Mickey snarled. His eyes were raging as though he had just caught his lover cheating.

"Pshh. Why? Looking for a late-night booty call? I don't think so. You ain't getting any more of this sweet ass. Not now, not ever!" Seth swayed back and forth as he gestured with his arms, convinced that his movements were making sense.

"What?" Mickey looked at Seth, confused. "I'm not here to fuck."

"Then why . . . are you here?" The ground beneath him continued to sway as he tried to focus on Mickey's nose.

"I was worried about you. You sounded drunk as fuck and I was worried that some guy would try and take advantage of you," Mickey blurted out, still angry but now more concerned.

Seth stopped swaying and stared at Mickey. "Worried

about me? You don't even like me. Go home, straight boy. Find some other pussy to fuck tonight, cuz I'm . . . I'm . . ." Seth swayed back and forth as he watched the world around him flip before everything went black.

CHAPTER 16 – Seth

"Don't worry, you'll like it. No one has to know. My wife won't be back till Tuesday. It's not like it's the first time you've sucked a dick before. Think of it as one of your hookups. Just you and I blowing our loads. Come on. It's just a bit of fun . . . "

Seth's head jerked up as panic pulled him from his nightmare.

"Oww." The sudden movement sent a jolt of pain slicing through his head. "What the heck . . . ?"

Throbbing pain hammered his head every time he attempted to move. His throat was sore, and his legs were freezing.

Slowly, Seth opened his eyes. He was sitting on the floor, clinging to the toilet in nothing but his Riddler underwear.

Classy. Real classy, Seth.

Ignoring the shooting pain, his eyes focused on the piece of material draped across the bathroom sink.

His shirt. The one he wore last night.

Covered in vomit.

Great . . .

Laying on the floor, next to the sink, were soiled paper towels. Most likely from cleaning up more of his puke.

Classy, man. Real fucking classy.

He looked around but didn't see his jeans. Perhaps he took them off before he came into the bathroom.

Seth closed his eyes as another wave of nausea overtook him. He breathed in and out, trying to concentrate on anything other than the desire to bend over the toilet and let it all out.

He felt like he was dying. Seriously, how many shots did he have last night? He could barely remember the bar, let alone the strip club. He hoped he still had some cash in his wallet. Otherwise, it was going to be a very cheap week.

Seth's head jolted when he heard the sound of heavy breathing directly behind him. He instantly regretted the sudden movement as a wave of nausea came crashing down on him.

Laying in his bathtub, fast asleep, was Mickey. Seth's heart began to race.

The Irish beefcake lay shirtless, in nothing but his designer ripped jeans. His red and black hair, which was normally slicked back, now fell roughly at both sides of his face, giving him a rough rocker-biker vibe.

Seth tried not to laugh at the sight of Mickey's large body crammed into his tiny tub. His head tilted forward uncomfortably as a tiny stream of drool made its way from the corner of his mouth to his perfectly sculpted chest.

He watched as Mickey's chest rose and fell with each breath. The poor guy looked so uncomfortable crammed in that tub.

Why was he here?

Then, memory set in. Mickey had been waiting for him when he came home last night . . . piss drunk.

Shit. Did that mean Mickey had watched as Seth prayed to the porcelain gods?

Great.

Nothing gave a man a boner more than watching fluid project out of another man's mouth.

Kiss me, baby, I'm gorgeous.

Mickey's body jerked in the tub as his sleepy eyes parted. He looked around, confused until his eyes fell on Seth. He jerked upright with nothing but concern in his eyes. "Shit. You, okay?"

Seth nodded and grimaced.

"Take it your head's poundin'?"

"Yeah, like a bitch," Seth moaned as he closed his eyes and rested his head on the toilet once again. His eyes popped open when he realized where his head was resting. He moved to prop himself up against the wall instead.

The two stared at each other in silence. Seth sat on the floor while Mickey sat in the tub.

"So, how bad was I last night?" Seth asked, fearing the answer.

"Well, after you passed out in front of your building . . . "

"I passed out?" Seth's eye widened.

"Yeah, you dropped like a ton of bricks. Smacked your face against the concrete pretty good."

Seth realized his jaw was sore as well. That explained that mystery.

"Then I carried your scrawny ass up to your apartment, where I had to balance your unconscious body over my shoulder while I tried to fish your keys out of your skinny jeans."

Seth didn't like the way this story was going. Perhaps he should count his losses and just jump out the window.

"Oh, but the real fun started when we got into your apartment, and you decided to rejoin the world of the living. You were furious that I was in your apartment, so you began punching my chest until your body decided to show me just how much you hated my guts by projectile vomiting all over my Tom Ford shirt."

"Oh god." Seth placed his head in his hands and waited to die.

"Once I removed my shirt, I tried to convince you to lay down in bed, at which point you thought it was a good time to describe in detail all the ways in which you were going to make me come. Number six is my favorite by the way." Mickey gave Seth a cocky smirk. "That is when your body suddenly realized it wasn't done reenacting *The Exorcist*, but thankfully this time you managed to make it to the toilet with only minimal backsplash."

"Oh my god, I want to die. Please stop talking. Leave now and forget you ever met my sad face."

"But it's such a cute face."

Seth felt his cheeks begin to flush.

"I tried to clean you up as best I could, then I decided to camp out with you in the bathroom."

Seth wanted to crawl into a hole and die. "I'm so sorry for being such a dumbass last night."

"It was fine."

"Why didn't you just go sleep in my bed? It couldn't have been comfortable sleeping in that tiny tub."

"You kept puking, and I was worried you might choke on your own vomit, so I wanted to keep an eye on you. Most of the night you just slept with your face on the toilet seat, but I guess I fell asleep there toward the end." Mickey looked like he was disappointed in himself.

Seth couldn't believe Mickey had spent the night taking care of him. Watching out for him and keeping him safe. Why? Seth was nothing more than a one-night stand. It didn't make any sense.

But to be honest, that was the sweetest thing anyone had ever done for him. No one had ever spent the night watching over him while he was sick. Making sure he was safe and okay. His heart expanded in his chest.

Seth pulled himself up off the cold tiles and walked over to where Mickey lay crunched in the bathtub. He knelt down and gently kissed the side of Mickey's cheek. "Thank you for taking care of me last night."

Mickey stared up at Seth with his deep emerald eyes. "No problem, sweet cheeks. It was my pleasure." He gave Seth a slight smile that was more appreciative of Seth's *thank you*, than trying to be smug.

Perhaps there was more there than a simple one-night stand. Seth extended his hand. "How about you go lay down in my bed and get some rest? I want to hop in the shower and wash off this grossness."

Mickey's bare chest brushed against Seth's arm as he exited the bathroom. The man knew how to flirt, that's for sure.

Fifteen minutes later, Seth emerged from the shower, wrapped in nothing but a towel. Feeling halfway human again, he followed the delicious smell of freshly made pancakes.

Mickey stood by the stove, shirtless, flipping pancakes

as if he owned the place. Seth's eyes fell on the massive demon tattoo that covered the majority of Mickey's back. The image was terrifying. The eyes seemed to follow you as you moved about the room.

Seth wondered what the significance of the tattoo meant for Mickey. Was it simply an intimidation tactic? Or did it serve some meaningful purpose?

As if they had a mind of their own, Seth's eyes locked onto Mickey's perfectly formed bubble butt which was currently protected by his faded designer jeans.

How many times a day does this guy work out? Seth admired the insanely fit physique of the Irish stud standing before him. The guy must eat nothing but chicken and broccoli to maintain such a fit body.

As if sensing a disturbance in the force, Mickey glanced over his shoulder. "All washed up? Hope you're hungry, sweet cheeks." He plated the last of the pancakes, then grabbed the orange juice from the fridge. He poured them both a glass and then passed Seth a plate, nodding toward the couch. "Go, sit down, and eat. I'll join you in a sec."

"You do realize this is my apartment, right?"

"Yes, and you do realize that I don't ask people to do things twice. Don't make me sic Patrick on you." Mickey winked as he grabbed the maple syrup and followed Seth into the living room.

He scootched onto the couch next to Seth, legs touching.

"Loving this towel look on you." Mickey smirked as he passed Seth the maple syrup.

"Yeah, well, someone ordered me to sit, so I didn't exactly have time to throw on a pair of shorts."

"Smart man."

The devilish grin on Mickey's face had Seth wondering what was going on.

Was Mickey bi? His actions last night, and then again this morning, indicated he was interested in him. So why the sudden freak out the last time they hooked up?

Seth passed the syrup back to Mickey, who proceeded to pour half the bottle on his pancakes. Seth could barely remember what the pancakes had looked like under the mound of maple syrup.

"So, are you going to tell me why you called me last night while I was out with the guys?"

"Mmm. Oh, yeah," Mickey mumbled as he swallowed a mouth full of pancake. "My inside gal at the NYPD got a peek at the toxicology reports for the guys on my crew who died, and she found something interesting. All three guys had high levels of lysergic acid diethylamide in their blood at the time of their deaths."

Seth sat there with a confused look on his face.

"LSD. It's a potent hallucinogen. When exposed, it makes people hallucinate, have terrifying thoughts, and feelings of despair. It can make the person feel like they are going insane." Mickey took another bite of his pancakes.

"So you think they were all drug users?" Seth asked, trying to make the connections.

Mickey shook his head. "No. Beep and Sven were drug users, but not Bernard. His old man was a drug addict, so he never touched the stuff. One of the guys who was with Beep the night he died, said that before Beep went crazy on the roof, he snorted some new drug he had never seen before. He said it was a purple powder that some drug dealer had given Beep.

"Akeil didn't take a hit, since he didn't know who the drug dealer was. Rule number one: Only accept drugs from people you know." Mickey turned back to eating his pancakes.

Seth digested what he had just said.

Seth pulled his iPad out of his knapsack that rested next to the couch and began adding this new information to his case file.

"Is that your file? About my crew?"

Seth blushed as he stopped typing. "Yeah. It helps me keep things organized. I'm a visual learner, so it helps if I can see all the information in front of me. I'll see what I can find out about this drug and do some more research on LSD. I'm not really a drug user, so I don't know much about it."

"Well, if you need info on street drugs, you can always speak with Braden. He's our drug aficionado.

"You do realize that selling drugs is a major part of my

business, right?" Mickey commented.

Seth placed the iPad on the coffee table and took another bite of his breakfast. Frustrated, he finally turned to glare at Mickey.

Mickey continued enjoying his meal in peace.

Eventually, Seth's eyes burrowed into Mickey's gorgeous face.

"What?" Mickey finally asked, looking at Seth.

"I gotta ask—what the fuck is going on here?" Seth asked. His heart was racing but he would rather know the truth than let his mind wander.

"Going on where?"

"Don't play dumb. Here. You. Me. What is this? Why did you show up at my apartment last night pissed out of your mind?"

Mickey ignored his questions and continued to chow down on his food.

"Okay, answer me this. Are you gay? Straight?"

"Well, I did fuck you the other night," Mickey commented, refusing to look at Seth.

"Yeah, then you also freaked out and tried to sneak out of here before I woke up like you regretted having sex with me. By the way, thanks for that. Made me feel real fucking special," Seth's voice began to rise the angrier he got.

Mickey turned to face him. His eyes looked pained, as

though he were struggling against himself. "I never meant to make you feel bad. I did have a good time with you. Probably the best I've had in ages, but honestly, what difference does it make? Nothing can come of it, so why would I hang around the next morning?"

His words cut deep. Seth got his answer. He was just a one-night stand to Mickey. Nothing more. Why was he surprised?

Seth could feel his eyes beginning to water. He needed Mickey to leave before he broke down in front of him. "Thanks for breakfast and thanks for taking care of me last night, but I need you to leave now."

Mickey's mouth dropped open as he stared into Seth's hurt eyes. Mickey leaned in and took Seth's face in both his hands. "Look. I'm not saying that you don't mean anything to me. I find you sexy as fuck and sweet as candy. But you need to understand something about me.

"I'm Mickey O'Brien, next in line to take over my father's criminal organization. I'm bi. I fuck lots of women and occasionally fuck guys on the down-low. What do you think would happen if I walked into my club holding your hand in front of my crew? I would lose their respect and my father would shoot me in the head.

"There's no future with me. I'm a criminal. I hurt people. I do bad things, and I can't be the guy you deserve. That's why I tried to sneak out of here the other night. Because I knew if I stayed, I wouldn't want to leave."

Seth sat in shock. He had never expected Mickey to be

so open and forthcoming. Guys like Mickey were always closeted and kept everything a secret. They never opened up or shared their true feelings with anyone. To open up was a sign of weakness. A show of vulnerability.

But Mickey's words were true. What sort of life could they have together? Did he really want to date a criminal? Was he willing to be in a relationship and love this man from the shadows?

"And the reason I came here last night, was because I was worried about you. You sounded drunk as fuck, and I didn't want you fucking some other dude. So, yeah, I guess I was also a little jealous." Mickey had removed his hands from Seth's face and was now gently caressing Seth's thigh.

Seth let out a breath as he tried to make sense of everything. Part of him wanted Mickey, to see where this could go, but part of him was hesitant. He knew this would be an uphill battle.

"Look. I don't know how I feel about anything you just said. Part of me is flattered, part of me is angry, and part of me is just confused." Seth placed his hand on top of Mickey's and began caressing it with his thumb. "What is it that you want to happen?"

Mickey's emerald green eyes looked conflicted and unsure. It was clear he was battling between the hyper-masculine bravado he had to portray and the hidden desires he was feeling within. Seth could not imagine how hard that turmoil must be on the soul.

"I honestly don't fucking know. I want you. I don't want anyone else to have you. But I also can't be with you. How fucked up is that?" Mickey leaned back on the couch, tilting his head upward to stare at the ceiling.

Seth's heart went out to the guy. Mickey was in so much emotional pain. He needed time to figure this out.

"How about this?" Seth placed his hand on Mickey's leg as he waited for Mickey to face him. "We take things slow. You and I can hang out occasionally and get to know each other. We can be discreet and hang out in places you are comfortable with. Whenever you are around your crew, I will be 'Seth, the guy looking into your friend's death.' When we are in private, we can be 'Mickey and Seth, sex-crazed maniacs.'" Seth let out a chuckle.

He wasn't sure if opening himself up to this possibility was such a good idea, but he was starting to like the guy and wasn't ready to give it all up yet. He wanted to get to know this complex Prince of the Criminal Underworld more.

Perhaps his heart would hate him later, but Seth had to give this a shot.

"Are you really willing to do that? Be discreet and pretend nothing is going on when around my crew?" Mickey's eyes seemed hopeful as they searched for confirmation.

"Yeah. I figure we give it a try and if things don't work out, we walk away." Seth gave him a slight smile, trying to reassure Mickey that this was what he wanted. In reality, part of him was trying to convince himself as well.

"But if we do this, I have one, non-negotiable demand," Mickey said, with a serious look on his face. "You don't get to sleep with any other guys. You belong to me. And only I get to fuck you. Is that clear?"

Seth smirked. He liked this possessiveness.

Now he understood why not telling Mickey where he was last night had made him so mad. It was not knowing whether he was out fucking someone else that had driven him insane.

"I can do that but the same goes for you. No other guy or girl is allowed to touch that cock of yours. That dick belongs to me now, and if I find out you fucked anyone else, this arrangement is over, and I'll have my own pit bull come after you."

Mickey grinned. "You have your own pit bull?"

"I have friends who would love to hurt any guy who breaks my heart. The less you know, the better."

"Sounds like a deal."

"Perfect."

Seth got up and straddled Mickey's thick thighs. He leaned in and gently kissed his rough lips. Mickey opened his mouth and let his tongue slide into Seth's.

He moaned. Fuck. Mickey was such a hot slab of beef. Seth could feel his cock hardening under the towel.

Mickey's lips turned upward as he let out a chuckle.

"Someone's getting excited," Mickey noted, pulling his lips from Seth's.

"What can I say, I'm horny and you're hot as fuck." Seth attacked Mickey's lips once again, hoping to get Mickey to take this to the bedroom.

Mickey pulled away, smiling. "Before you get me too hard, I need to jet."

Seth's mouth dropped open, hurt and offended.

"It's not that I don't want to bury my face in your ass for an hour or two. The guys and I run a football or 'soccer' camp as you Americans like to call it, for some kids in the neighborhood. I gotta be at the park in an hour."

Seth was surprised by this revelation. This was the first time he had been cockblocked by underprivileged children. Would it make him a bad person if he got upset? Probably.

He could live with this rejection.

Seth's face lightened. "Being rejected so you can help out kids . . . I think my ego can handle that one. Go. And thanks again for breakfast and last night." Seth climbed off Mickey and tried to ignore his tenting towel.

Mickey stood, adjusting his own tent, and leaned down for one last kiss. "Any time, sweet cheeks. I'll call you later."

Seth's heart filled with the promise of his words. Mickey turned and gave Seth one last smile before walking out the door.

CHAPTER 17 - Seth

The rest of the afternoon was spent combing through case files and trying to piece together the events that transpired on the night of each death.

Bernard, the first victim, had been unloading a truck at one of their warehouses. He was simply carrying boxes from the truck outside and stacking them against a wall inside.

Witnesses said they didn't see anything unusual until Bernard came running out of the warehouse in a panic. People tried to help him, but he kept shouting, claiming that something was in the warehouse trying to kill him. His eyes were dilated, and he was sweating profusely.

It all came to a tragic end when Bernard ran screaming into traffic, not noticing the oncoming truck that plowed right into him. People said it was like watching a watermelon explode.

The crew checked the warehouse, but the only thing they found was an empty aerosol can with some purple residue around the rim.

Sven, on the other hand, had a much more violent end. Those who witnessed the horrific event noted that Sven's behavior had been normal, up until he went to use the washroom. When he returned, he was acting paranoid, accusing everyone of stealing his stash. Paranoia turned to aggression when Sven became convinced that people had stolen his money, and that his drug dealer was on his way to the bar to kill him.

The look of sheer terror in his eyes, had some patrons believing someone was on their way to murder him. It was during one of these scuffles that Sven was able to grab hold of someone's gun.

The room watched in horror as a terrified Sven placed the gun to his temple and pulled the trigger.

It took the crew two days to completely wipe the blood and brain matter off the walls of the pub. For a month, everyone in the bar refused to sit in the booth where much of Sven's brains had landed.

Then of course there was Jasper Murphy, aka Beep. The third and final victim. The boy was only twenty-one when he decided to take a swan dive off the roof of a building. The only other witness that night claimed Jasper had snorted some purple powder shortly before going crazy.

So, what was the connection?

All three men worked for the O'Briens.

All three men seemed normal at the beginning but then turned paranoid and aggressive.

And in two of the three cases, there was an unknown purple substance found at the scene.

Seth had reviewed the case with Marc, who suggested he speak with a professor, Dr. Maleo, at Columbia University, regarding the purple substance. Marc had been able to procure the exact chemical formula of the powder from one of his contacts at the NYPD and hoped the professor might be able to shed some light on the compound.

They weren't able to get a meeting with the professor directly, but he suggested they meet his teaching assistant, Miss Sabrina Caine. Caine had agreed to meet with Seth Monday after classes. Until then, he had lots to do.

Seth was just about to make himself a cup of tea when there was an abrupt knock at the door. Annoyed by the sudden interruption, Seth peeked through the peephole and rolled his eyes.

"*Ouvre la porte*," commanded the voice of an impatient woman.

Seth groaned as he turned the lock and opened the door. "*Bonjour, Grand-mère.*"

"You look like shit," his grandmother proclaimed as she pushed her 5'2 frame through the door and sauntered past him.

Seth closed the door and followed her into his tiny living room. He watched as she took inventory of the decrepit state of his living conditions and awaited her judgment.

The woman might be tiny, but she had a commanding presence. "Make me some tea, then come sit with me on this . . . is it a *chaise*?" The woman turned her nose up at Seth as if the couch had offended her.

Seth rolled his eyes and turned toward the kitchen. "No, it's not a *chair*, Gran . . . it's a couch." She had been here all of thirty seconds, and he was already hating his life.

"If you say so." She pulled a tissue from her expensive purse and began wiping down the offensive item.

Seth smirked. If she only knew what he really did on that couch, she would have used a blow torch to clean it off.

Clarisa Dubois was a woman of refined breeding. Having grown up in Paris, she was used to the highest quality food, service, and fashion. She demanded respect and above all, obedience from her family. While she expected a lot, she was also a kind woman when it came to matters of the heart.

Seth had been close to his grandmother growing up and she had been the first person he came out to.

It pained him when he realized that in his rush to sever his life from his parents, he had inadvertently severed his relationship with his gran as well.

Seth passed his grandmother her cup of tea and sat

down next to her on the couch. Her Chanel suit was freshly pressed and her legs were crossed at the ankles.

"So, you decided to live here, in this dump, instead of with your parents or in my downtown condo," her French accent added an offensive harshness to her words while her hands waved off the offending items.

"It's not like that," Seth attempted before he was silenced by his gran's raised hand.

"What is the nonsense going on between you and your parents?"

Seth placed his mug back on the coffee table and tucked his leg under his butt. "Nothing, Gran. It's between me and them."

"Don't give me that shit. When you stop showing up at Christmas and Thanksgiving, it is my business!"

Seth knew there was no getting out of his grandmother's interrogations. Once Gran got her claws into something, she never let go. Resisting was useless.

"What it all boils down to is Mom and Dad choosing to believe a stranger's lies over the word of their son. I refuse to live with people who chose power over family." Seth refused to shed any more tears for the parents who turned their backs on him. "I would rather live here, on my own, than with them."

His grandmother looked at him lovingly, as she gently touched the side of his face. He leaned into the unexpected soft touch, craving the warmth and affection it promised.

"*Mon Cheri*. I don't know what happened between you and your parents, but you will always have my love. Family comes first and I will always believe anything you tell me. So please, tell me what it is."

The love in his heart grew with the sincerity of his gran's words. While his grandmother may appear tough and strict, she really did have a gentle heart.

"It's nothing, Gran. It's between them and me."

Seth could be stubborn and would not open up to someone unless he wanted to. Having experienced his strong will before, she appeared to put this aside for the time being.

With that in mind, she placed her hand on Seth's leg and gave it a gentle pat, then added, "I will speak with your mother and set her straight. But until then, promise you'll come and visit me in Manhattan? I don't have many years left on this earth, and I want to spend as many of them with my favorite grandson. Even if he is a flaming queen."

"Gran!" Seth shouted, pretending to be offended.

She smiled at him as he stood up from the couch. Seth walked his grandmother to the door.

"Will you be all right heading home?"

"Oh, yes. Marco is standing outside guarding the Bentley. I feel like Whitney Huston every time that man helps me out of my car."

"You look just as fabulous, Gran."

Perfectly manicured fingers patted Seth's cheeks as his fabulous gran left his apartment.

From his apartment window, Seth watched as his grandmother stepped into her car and sped off to her penthouse on the Upper Westside. The woman had class, that's for sure.

As he bent down to remove the empty mugs from the coffee table, something caught his eye. An envelope had been partially tucked under one of the books he had been reading.

He pulled out the mysterious envelope and peeked inside. His heart stopped in his chest.

Seth pulled a check out of the envelope and stared at the figures—five thousand dollars. He couldn't believe his gran had left him so much money.

He felt his eyes begin to tear. Having this money gave him so much breathing room. While he wasn't broke, he was on a very tight budget. Having this money available meant he could stop skipping meals during the week and not constantly worry if he would have enough money to pay all his bills.

He loved Eve to death but putting together her bachelorette party had been an expense he couldn't afford. Seth knew this was a one-time event, and he was happy to make the sacrifices so she could have a memorable evening. But having this money in his hands, provided Seth with a sense of relief he didn't even know had been an issue.

Seth picked up his phone and called his grandmother quickly.

"Hello?"

"Thank you, Gran. You don't know how much that means to me." Seth was trying not to cry on the phone. He didn't want her to worry, but he also wanted to give her kind gesture the recognition it deserved.

"You're welcome, sweetie. Always know that I love you."

With those powerful words, Seth hung up the phone and let the tears stream down his face. Perhaps he wasn't as alone in the world as he thought.

Standing in the middle of such history and grandeur was extremely intimidating. The number of famous and brilliant minds that roamed these hallways was so inspiring when you thought about it.

At any moment you might be walking past the next great thinker or even president. Who knew which one of these students would create the next lifesaving drug or find a cure for cancer?

Within these walls, anything was possible.

After getting lost twice, Seth was finally able to locate the small office belonging to Professor Maleo's teaching assistant, Ms. Sabrina Caine.

"Come in," a friendly voice called from the other side

of the door.

Seth gently pushed the door open and popped his head in. "Ms. Caine?"

"Yes, that's me. You must be Mr. Richards. Please, come in."

The woman appeared to be in her early thirties with long black hair pulled back in a tight ponytail. She pulled off her thin-framed glasses as she made her way around the mahogany desk to greet Seth. Her body seemed to glide as she moved around the desk.

The woman was a knock-out. She was tall, slender, and had the fiercest blue eyes Seth had ever seen. Seth was taken aback. He had been expecting a less attractive woman . . . perhaps short, glasses, frizzy hair . . . maybe chewing on a pencil? So, he was caught off guard by the woman's beauty.

"It's a pleasure to meet you." She shook Seth's hand and gestured toward the empty chair by her desk.

"I really appreciate you taking the time to see me today, especially on such short notice."

"Well, I was surprised when Dr. Maleo called me yesterday requesting the meeting. It's not often that your boss calls you personally on a Sunday with an urgent request. Must be important. So here I am." She gave Seth a smile that seemed a bit forced.

Seth got the feeling she hadn't exactly volunteered to step in for Dr. Maleo.

"Once again, I *am* sorry about that, but it is kind of an urgent matter."

Ms. Caine leaned forward on her desk, giving Seth her undivided attention. "So, what is it that I can do for you?"

Seth swallowed hard, trying to ignore the growing nerves inside his stomach. The woman was brilliant. She was a Columbia TA, in Chemistry of all things.

Suddenly, Seth felt like a four-year-old, staring up at his mother, hoping she approved of his drawing.

He reached into his bag and pulled out the notepad he had written the chemical formula in. Seth slid the pad over to Ms. Caine and watched as she studied the equation.

"I was wondering if you could tell me a bit about this formula?"

Seth watched as Ms. Caines' eyes flew across the writing, studying each of the bonds and elements. He had seen that same expression before on Marc when he was calculating information, trying to figure out what information meant and how it could be used.

It was eerie to watch. The person was there, but they also weren't there. Their body was present, but their mind was off in a different realm.

Eyes returning to the land of the living, she glanced at Seth. "Where did you come across such a formula?"

"Umm, it's part of an ongoing investigation. Sorry, I can't share more details with you." It was better to keep what he knew to himself. He didn't need people asking questions or getting in his way.

She looked over her glasses as if studying Seth's face.

What was she searching for?

"Hmm. Well, without much information, I can tell you that this is the formula for a chemical compound."

"Yes, but what kind of chemical compound?"

"The base of this formula is lysergic acid diethylamide." When Seth didn't react, she added, "LSD. LSD is a potent drug that causes extreme hallucinations. It can alter a person's perception of reality, causing them to experience terrifying thoughts and despair. It distorts the senses, so people believe what they are seeing is real. If not taken under a safe and controlled environment, the results could be . . . deadly."

Seth felt queasy, imagining the nightmares those men must have experienced. The nightmare was terrifying enough for the person to choose death rather than live another moment of their ordeal.

Ms. Caine studied Seth's reaction, appearing to enjoy the discomfort Seth was experiencing. After a moment, she added, "There are also a few other additives to this formula."

"What do you mean?" Seth asked, scooching forward in his chair.

"Whoever created this, wanted to boost the intensity of the hallucination and speed up its effects. LSD is potent enough on its own, but when you combine it with these other additives, the user has virtually no chance of survival.

"If the hallucinations don't drive the user mad, the user's heart rate will continue to increase, until the person eventually suffers a massive heart attack. This drug was designed to kill." The woman stared at Seth with intensity.

Seth found it hard to swallow. His mouth was suddenly very dry. Whoever had created this drug was clearly out for revenge. This was no accident. Someone wanted these guys to suffer before they died.

The woman slid the notepad back across the desk. "I really hope you catch this guy. This drug was designed to kill, and I pity any person who comes in contact with it."

As Seth reached for the notepad his eyes fell on the tiny tattoo hidden against the inside of Ms. Caine's wrist. It was a simple tattoo: a red rose with barbed wire running around the stem.

Seth admired the tattoo for a moment. The intricate design and attention to detail were stunning. The interlocking petals of the flower and sharpness of the thorns seemed to bring the rose to life. Whoever the tattoo artist was had taken great pride in their work.

Sensing his gaze on her hidden gem, Ms. Caine pulled the cuff of her shirt down, removing the tattoo from his sight.

"Thanks again for your time, Ms. Caine. This information will really help." Seth shook the woman's hand, then made his way out of her office.

Someone had created a drug designed to kill and was using it to murder members of Mickey's crew.

What had they gotten themselves into?

CHAPTER 18- Mickey

It had been two days since Mickey had spent the night sleeping in Seth's bathtub. That night, he had been worried about Seth and wanted to make sure he was still breathing while Seth slept on the floor. For some reason, the coolness of the tiles seemed to make Seth feel better, so Mickey didn't argue.

Mickey had spent the night rubbing Seth's back while he lay passed out on the floor. It was the first time ever that Mickey wanted to be there for someone. Take care of them. Help them feel better and keep them safe.

When asked about that night, he tried to downplay the level of attention he had given Seth. Seth already felt embarrassed enough as it was, plus, showing that level of affection wasn't exactly boner material. Men were supposed to be strong and not show emotion.

If his father had seen the way Mickey tenderly took

care of Seth, he would have taken him behind the shed and torn him a new one.

Even though they hadn't been able to see each other over the past two days, they had spoken on the phone briefly Monday night and spent the rest of the time randomly texting each other.

Mickey couldn't help the stupid grin that took over his face whenever his phone vibrated with a new incoming text from Seth. Even the random messages that served no purpose made Mickey smile—he didn't need to know that Seth had finished doing the dishes, but for some reason, he found it fascinating when mentioned by his little tiger.

It was clear that Seth was also using these messages as an opportunity to also get to know Mickey. Random questions such as what his favorite movie was or which side of the bed he preferred to sleep on kept popping in between the sea of messages being received.

To each of these messages, Mickey immediately responded, trying not to make it obvious while around the guys. Apparently, he would make a horrible spy.

Patrick kept eyeing him. Mickey tried to play it off as nothing, but he knew he wasn't fooling his best friend.

When had he gotten so soft?

Mickey was never like this. He had hook-ups, fuck friends, and occasionally dated. In all these years, he'd never given a shit when someone sent him a message and most certainly did not respond unless it was something important.

There was something different about Seth. Somehow, he had been enchanted by his charm and had been turned into a jealous, obsessive, needy man.

Man . . . the guys were going to kick his ass if they ever saw him acting this way.

There was a certain vulnerability and uncertainty Seth kept hidden under a veil of confidence. Every once in a while, that mask would slip and Mickey would get a glimpse of the real Seth, the one Seth kept hidden from the world. The one Mickey hoped only he would see.

By Tuesday afternoon, Mickey realized the reason Seth had been sending so many 'random' texts was that he was trying to maintain contact with him. What was the saying? "Out of sight, out of mind." Given Seth's insecurities, it made sense that he would want to keep as much contact as possible.

Mickey got the feeling that until they figured out what 'this' was between them, Seth would not feel settled.

If he was being honest with himself, he kind of missed seeing Seth's face as well—even if it had only been two days. God, what was happening to him?

Mickey pulled out his cell and texted Seth:

M: *Tonight, 7 PM. Wear something comfortable.*

S: *Oooo . . . sounds mysterious. Comfortable as in sweatpants? Or comfortable as in birthday suit?*

Mickey smirked at the thought of Seth answering the door in nothing but a tie. Yum.

M: *Comfy as in walking clothes. No one gets to see your bday suit but me [devil face emoji].*

"What's got you smiling like a cheerleader in the backseat of a quarterback's car?"

Mickey shoved his phone back in his pocket and smirked at his best friend.

"Nothing, Paddy. Just a message from Seth."

"The kid looking into the Purple Dust?"

They had begun referring to the purple drug as "Purple Dust" when someone commented that it looked like dust you could snort.

"Yeah, that guy." Mickey averted his gaze.

He and Patrick never lied to each other, so he hated not being forthcoming with what was really going on.

"Nice kid," Patrick said, shaking his head in agreement before turning to head back into the warehouse.

That was the nice thing about Patrick, he never pushed Mickey for information. He always knew Mickey would tell him when he was ready.

Now, Mickey just had to make one quick stop before their date tonight.

♣ ♣ ♣

Seth was already waiting on the front steps of his apartment building when Mickey pulled up. His head snapped up at the sound of the Maserati approaching.

Mickey felt his heart warm when he saw the excited look on Seth's face as he approached. How many people can say they have a special someone who looks at them with such excitement in their eyes? He loved this feeling.

Mickey rolled down the passenger side window as Seth approached the car.

"How much for an hour?" he shouted, smiling as two elderly women turned their heads in shock.

"Not sure you can handle this much hotness," Seth responded, leaning in the car window suggestively.

Mickey smirked. The boy was playful.

"How about you hop in, and we'll see if I can convince you otherwise."

Seth winked and hopped in the car. His face lit up when Mickey passed him a small box wrapped in green tissue paper.

"What's this?"

"Just a little something for you." Mickey gave Seth a bashful nod. "Nothing too exciting."

Seth's face gleamed. He tore back the tissue paper and turned over the box to remove the lid. Seth let out a gasp when he caught sight of the leather bracelet he had been eyeing at the vendors' market the other day. He pulled the item out slowly and turned it over in his hand. It was the exact same bracelet he had been looking at the other day.

"Oh my god. You went back and bought this bracelet

for me?" Seth asked, still in shock.

He could feel his cheeks flush. "Yeah, well, you said you liked it. And I figured it would look great on you." Mickey wasn't used to someone giving him this much attention for something he tried to brush off as no big deal.

"I . . . Wow . . . You didn't . . . Mickey, I love it. Thank you so much!" He leaned forward and wrapped his arms around Mickey's neck.

Mickey closed his eyes and enjoyed the sweet scent of Seth's body and how good it felt pressed against his.

Seth pulled away and gazed at his present. "This is the sweetest thing anyone has ever done for me."

Mickey smiled. He loved seeing Seth so happy. He wanted to make Seth smile like this every day.

"Here, let me help you put it on." Mickey took the bracelet and fastened the straps around Seth's soft skin. "There. Looks great on you."

Lifting his arm, Seth admired his new piece of jewelry.

Mickey's heart warmed. He hoped to have many other opportunities to shower Seth with gifts. He deserved to be taken care of and made to feel special.

"Thanks. It looks amazing." Seth slid his hand into Mickey's and clipped his seatbelt with his other. "So, where are we going?" Seth asked, excitement plastered across his face.

"It's a surprise. I kind of missed you and wanted to see

your pretty face."

Seth's face beamed hearing those words. Seth's grip tightened as Mickey sped off with a screech of his tires.

They arrived at their destination thirty minutes later. The air was warm and the sky was clear. It was a perfect night to walk the grounds of Coney Island.

"You brought me to Coney Island?" Seth cried out, excited as ever.

Mickey swore he saw Seth do a little excited bounce in his seat.

"Hope that's all right?"

"Of course! I love rides and games. I have not been here in years. Not since my gran brought me when I was a kid with my mom."

Mickey couldn't help but notice the sudden change in demeanor at the mention of his mother.

"Do your parents live in Jersey as well?"

"No, they live back in Chicago. I don't speak with them anymore."

Mickey's eyes widened with this sudden revelation. "How come?"

Seth looked out the window as they approached the large Ferris wheel. "Long story. My gran lives in Manhattan, so I guess I have some family close by."

Mickey decided not to press the subject. Clearly, Seth

was not comfortable discussing the complicated relationship he had with his parents.

For the first time, Mickey felt a tinge of disappointment that he had not yet earned that level of trust.

And how could he? They'd just barely met.

He parked the car, then they made their way along the boardwalk, stopping at each booth along the way. Seth was like a kid in a candy store. He insisted on playing each game they passed, and taste-tested every sample of food offered.

Mickey's heart flooded every time he heard Seth's warm laugh. There was so much happiness and spirit in him. He was the ray of sunshine that burst through the storm clouds in a gloomy sky. You couldn't help but smile and feel good in his presence.

His true test of patience came when he spent twenty minutes playing the ring toss bottle game until he was finally able to win Seth a *Sonic the Hedgehog* stuffed animal. Seth casually mentioned that *Sonic* was one of his all-time favorite games as a kid, so of course, Mickey was determined to win him the damn doll.

No matter how long it took or how much money he had to spend, he had to beat that fucking game. It was now becoming a matter of pride. Nobody wanted to fuck the loser. Potential mates always went for the winner in the pride.

Mickey had to prove to Seth that he could be his provider. He would win Seth that fucking hog, then spend the rest of the night shoving his own 'hog' between Seth's cheeks.

Truth be told, Mickey was contemplating just stealing the stuffed animal since the damn game had to be rigged. It was virtually impossible to get a tiny ring to rest on the neck of a slippery bottle. You were set up to fail, so he was going to readjust the system.

By some fucking miracle, his last ring ended up staying in place, winning him the torturous doll. He had never felt so relieved.

Seth squealed as Mickey handed him his prized possession. Mickey's ego and pride remained intact.

The sky was dark by the time they walked toward the giant Ferris wheel. Mickey was looking forward to getting a little alone time with Seth up and away from watching eyes.

He hated not being able to hold Seth's hand in public or lean over and give him a kiss. But Mickey had a reputation to maintain. He could not be seen as some faggot or pansy when he had a crew to lead. Thankfully, Seth understood his need for discretion.

Mickey placed his hand discreetly on Seth's lower back as he helped him up into the seat. A moment later the wheel began to turn and the two were lifted toward the evening sky.

"Wow, look at that view." Seth's eyes were wide as he took in the view of the Brooklyn skyline. Streetlamps and traffic lights peppered the view below in a sea of white, red, and green flashing lights.

Mickey slid his hand over Seth's and placed them both in his lap. Seth smiled at the affectionate gesture.

"I've been waiting to do that all night," Mickey confessed.

"Me too," Seth replied, leaning into Mickey's warm body. "So, tell me about your childhood. What was little Mickey like growing up? Was he a hellion?" Seth chuckled.

As the wheel turned, Mickey opened up about his childhood. He began with his mother. How she had been a sweet and kind woman who was taken from them when he was just a boy. He mentioned his father's growing despair at the loss of his wife, his violent temper, and tough upbringing.

Then he found himself opening up about his friendship with Patrick. Having finally found the brother he always wanted. Both had abusive fathers, and both had grown up without their mothers.

Mickey couldn't believe how easy it was to open up to Seth and tell him things he would never consider telling another living soul.

"Is that why you and Patrick have similar looks and hairstyles?"

Mickey thought about that for a moment. They both had slicked-back undercuts, with two-toned hairs: black and red for Mickey and black and blue for Patrick.

"The hair is kind of our signature look. Since we both consider each other brothers we wanted something that connected us. And if you're talking about how our ripped bodies look the same, that's because we both work out together. We're basically on the same fitness routine, so we get the same results. But you have to admit, my body looks slightly sexier than Patrick's, right?" Mickey smirked as he lifted his shirt exposing his eight-pack abs.

Seth just shook his head, acknowledging that the man sitting beside him was an idiot.

"And what about the future? Will you take over when your father passes away?"

This was a topic that had been weighing on Mickey's mind for quite some time. He wanted to bring the family out of the shadows and move toward more legitimate endeavors. There was a lot of good they could do in the community, but people were hesitant to participate or invest when they realized Mickey and his crew were involved. People were always afraid of getting tangled up in illegal activities and scandals.

"That's a good question. Yes, I'll take over because the crew is my family and I have a responsibility to take care of everyone. I'm just not sure about how I want to run the business. I have some ideas about moving into more mainstream businesses but haven't mentioned any of this to my father yet."

"Well, from what I have seen so far, everyone seems to respect the fuck out of you." Seth leaned in and placed his head against Mickey's shoulder as their cart reached the top of the Ferris wheel.

The wheel stopped for a moment, presumably to let some passengers off below.

As their cart gently swayed, Mickey couldn't help but feel at peace. He liked the feeling of Seth's warm body pressed up against his. He liked that Seth took an interest in his future and his ideas.

This was the type of partner he wanted. Someone sweet and supportive. Someone he could tell his darkest secrets to and who wouldn't pass judgment.

Mickey placed his fingers under Seth's chin and slowly brought Seth's face up to his. He stared longingly into Seth's warm brown eyes and felt his heart begin to quicken.

Under the light of the stars and the gentle breeze of the ocean, Mickey leaned forward and kissed Seth's soft lips. The heat of passion and sparks of lust passed between their lips.

This was the perfect kiss.

This was the stuff romantic movies were made of.

Mickey lost himself in the warmth of Seth's lips.

A moment later, there was a jerk as the wheel began to turn once again.

Both men pulled away, staring lovingly into each other's eyes.

This was the beginning of something special.

And something complicated . . .

CHAPTER 19 – Seth

The Ferris wheel eventually came to a stop and the teenage worker helped Mickey and Seth off the ride. Seth laughed as he walked away from the Ferris wheel and headed toward a stand selling funnel cakes.

"Hey, do you want to grab a funnel cake?" Seth asked over his shoulder.

"Sure, I guess. I've never actually had one before."

"What? I feel like you've been deprived of a childhood. This cannot stand! Come on. My treat," Seth said as he grabbed Mickey's arm and tugged him toward the heavenly cakes.

"Mickey? Hey, boss!" a voice called from behind them.

Seth felt Mickey yank his arm quickly out of Seth's grip as he turned toward the voice.

"Oh, hey, Braden. What are you and Dom doing here?" Mickey's voice cracked as he took a few paces toward his friends.

Seth stood where he was, wondering whether he should approach the group or stay in his position. They hadn't discussed what was acceptable decorum when out in public.

"Oh, you know, checkin' shit out, teasin' the ladies," Braden spilled as he made obscene gestures with his hands and groin.

Mickey's shoulders seemed to tighten as if he were uncomfortable with the situation. Seth decided to stay where he was and let Mickey take the lead.

"So, what about you? You here with Paddy?" Braden asked, looking around for his brother in arms. "Oh, wait. Isn't that the dude Paddy had in the basement last week?"

Mickey glanced over his shoulder to where Seth was standing. "Ye—yeah. This is Seth. We ran into each other a few minutes ago. He is gonna do some work with Paddy. We were gonna go grab some food and chat strategy."

Seth noted the uncomfortableness in Mickey's voice. Mickey had been upfront about having to keep things on the down-low, but he wasn't even acknowledging Seth as his *friend*. He was simply a "guy working with Paddy." A nobody.

Seth couldn't help but feel the sting of rejection.

They were having such a wonderful date together, then

these buffoons showed up and ruined everything.

"Well, make sure you don't sit too close together. You don't want any chicks thinking you two are homos. Talk about being cock blocked, am I right?" Braden turned to his buddy expecting a high five, but his friend only shook his head, acknowledging that he was an idiot. "What?"

"Don't worry, man, we'll keep our distance," Mickey said with a bit of a chuckle.

Mickey's words stung. This was never going to work. How could he ever be happy if his boyfriend refused to acknowledge their relationship? Not that Mickey was his boyfriend, but the sentiment was the same.

Seth wanted a relationship where he could hold his man's hand in public. He wanted to be able to stop by his man's work and be acknowledged as his partner . . . His better half.

He didn't want a life of living in the shadows as someone's dirty little secret. That wasn't a relationship. That was a booty call.

How could he have been so stupid as to think this would ever work?

Mickey turned toward Seth and his face dropped when he saw the hurt in Seth's eyes.

Seth could feel his eyes moisten but refused to have a meltdown in front of these guys. He had already embarrassed himself enough in front of them.

He glanced down at his watch, then did the only thing

he could think of.

"Shit. Sorry, Mickey, just realized the time. I gotta jet. Got an early class tomorrow." Seth began taking a few steps backward as he watched the disappointment spread across Mickey's face. "You go have fun with your buddies. We can talk shop another time. It was nice running into you." These last words hurt to say, but he wanted to hurt Mickey, make him feel the sting of rejection just like he had.

Seth turned and walked toward the subway. He needed to get out of here.

"Seth! Wait!" Mickey called after him.

Seth didn't turn, for fear that Mickey would see the tears sliding down his cheeks. He quickened his pace, hoping Mickey was not following him.

How could he have been so stupid to think they could actually pull this off? That they could date in secret.

This was not the life he wanted. He didn't want to hide who he was just because someone else was too afraid to admit who they were.

He felt his chest tighten as all the hopes he had for a future with Mickey began to crash and burn. He could feel his heart breaking. Better now than later.

Seth stepped onto the subway platform and pulled his phone out of his pocket. There were already two text messages from Mickey. He didn't have the heart to read them, so he swiped left and deleted them without reading.

He powered off his cell phone and shoved it back into his pocket.

Mickey was the same as any other guy who let him down. He had survived them, and he will survive Mickey as well . . . Even if it hurt like hell.

♣ ♣ ♣

The next few days were spent ignoring Mickey's barrage of text messages and phone calls. Seth was not great with confrontation and quite frankly, didn't know what to say. It's not like Seth could get angry at the way Mickey handled the situation. He had been very clear and upfront about his need for discretion and keeping their activities under wraps. So, if Seth was angry at anyone, it would be himself for believing that he could have such a relationship.

Seth just needed some space to clear his head and give his heart time to wean itself off the drug that was Mickey.

Friday was Eve's big day. Seth was thankful for the distraction and a wedding was the perfect opportunity for him to lose himself, even if just for a few hours.

The wedding was perfect. Eve wore an elegant white, silk dress that draped to the floor. The eloquent beading of the bodice sparkled as she made her way down the aisle. A true beauty if he ever saw one.

Seth couldn't help but swallow the lump in his throat as James and Eve exchanged vows, promising to always love and respect one another, be that guiding hand through the dark times, always encourage and inspire one another, and finally, to always be that loving shoulder to lean on.

At the end of the vows, Seth felt that loneliness inside him grow. He wanted what Eve and James had, what Marc and Alex had.

Someone to grow old with. Someone who loved and protected him. Someone who inspired him and encouraged him to follow his dreams. Someone he could trust with his darkest secrets . . . and of course, someone who would believe him when he said his married boss was trying to sleep with him.

No matter how much he wanted it, that could never be Mickey. He let out a sigh, feeling sad and alone.

Sensing the sadness in his friend, Alex placed his hand on top of Seth's and gave it a squeeze. Perhaps Seth wasn't as alone as he thought.

He turned and gave Alex a weary smile. He was grateful Eve and Alex had welcomed him into their family. It was nice having friends who cared.

CHAPTER 20- Mickey

"You've been nothin' but a miserable twat all week. Snap out of it, Michele." Patrick knew how much Mickey hated being called by his birth name.

Mickey guessed that this was Patrick's way of soliciting a reaction and snapping him out of his mood.

"How about ya go fuck yerself?" Mickey snapped back, not bothering to look up from the couch he was lying on. His accent coming out stronger than usual, indicating that he was getting annoyed.

Mickey had been trying to apologize to Seth all week, but Seth kept ignoring his calls. He had even tried stopping by his apartment, but Seth refused to even answer the door.

The *bastard* made no attempt at pretending he wasn't home. He could hear the television blaring and Seth walking around the apartment, but Seth continued ignoring him for twenty minutes. Eventually, Mickey realized the stubborn twit was not going to acknowledge his presence, so he gave up and left.

Mickey felt horrible when he saw the rejected look on Seth's face when he didn't acknowledge him in front of his friends at Coney Island. The hurt and sadness in his eyes tore Mickey's heart apart.

But what was he supposed to do? He couldn't turn around and introduce Seth as the guy he was fuckin' and potentially dating. He had been very clear about what he could and could not offer Seth.

So why was he feeling so miserable?

Because you hurt the feelings of the guy you promised to protect. That's why.

Patrick chuckled as Mickey told him off.

"Wow, someone has really got ya by the balls."

Mickey shot his friend a quick glance from the couch. "That's the problem. I don't think they will be touchin' them ever again." Mickey avoided using pronouns as he didn't want to lie to his best friend.

He was pretty sure that Patrick caught on as he simply shook his head and didn't say anything.

"Well, if someone has got ya this upset, ya know they're worth fightin' for. You've never let anyone get this deep under your skin before. And if anyone can get this deep, they're someone I want standing beside you." Patrick walked to where Mickey lay sprawled on the couch and crouched down next to him. He placed his hand on

Mickey's bare chest and stared into his eyes. "Just know you can talk to me about anything. You know I'm always here for ya. And if there is anything I can do to help you fix things with . . . this miracle worker, you just say the word." Patrick gave Mickey one of his I'm-serious-and-you-can-always-count-on-me smiles.

Mickey nodded and gave him a half-smile. He knew Patrick always had his back, and he would never say anything or judge him for being in a relationship with a guy.

Patrick stood and walked back to the mini bar in the office and poured them both a whiskey. It was 11 AM, but no one gave a fuck.

Both jumped when the office door burst open and Mickey's father barged in. The bastard was looking particularly pissed off this morning.

"Hey, Pops, nice to see you." Mickey sat up, knowing he was about to get his ass pummeled.

Patrick stopped where he was, knowing not to get in the middle of father and son.

"What's this I hear about the Detroit delivery being late?" Clive barked as he stood, towering over his son.

Mickey rolled his eyes. "Relax, Pop. It was two days late. The driver had engine problems and had to get the engine fixed. It wasn't like he could just walk into an auto shop and get the repair done there. We had to send in Brody."

"That drunken prick? No wonder it took two fuckin'

days to get the shit fixed! I've got Manzini breathing down my neck wanting half his money back because the shipment was late, and he had to pay extra for his own delivery guys to wait around!"

Mickey rubbed the side of his arm. He hated it when his father treated him like an incompetent child. If it wasn't for his quick action, the shipment would not have made it at all as the engine was actually beyond repair. Brody just happened to have a spare engine in his shop that he was able to drive down to the site and switch out. Had he not had the engine available, the delivery never would have happened.

"Ya need to be smarter than this if you're going to take over one day. Ya need to have backup plans. Contingencies for when things go sideways. This is the only way you will stay in business and out of jail."

Clive could be a mean son of a bitch when things didn't go his way. Mickey knew better than to argue with his old man or try and explain.

"Sure thing, Pops. I'll do better next time." Mickey lowered his eyes, hating the feeling of not being good enough in his father's eyes.

His father was still glaring at him when a knock came on the office door.

"What?" Clive barked at whoever had the balls to interrupt his fatherly smackdown.

The door creaked open and one of the bartenders stuck their head in. "Sorry to interrupt, sir, but you have a package."

"Put it over there," Clive growled, nodding his head toward Mickey's desk.

The bartender dropped off the package and then scurried off.

"I'm not trying to be hard on ya, son, because I hate you," Clive continued as he walked over to the desk. "I'm just trying to prepare you so that you will be able to succeed when I'm gone and can't help you out."

Even when his father was trying to be nice, he sounded condescending.

Clive grabbed a knife off the desk and cut open the box that had been delivered without even checking who it was from. As he pulled back the flaps, a cloud of purple dust exploded into his face, catching him in his eyes, mouth, and nostrils.

Caught off guard, he gagged, sucking in a lung full of the purple particles.

"Dad!" Mickey shouted, jumping up from the couch and rushing toward his father.

Patrick stuck out his arm and clotheslined Mickey as he darted toward his dad. Mickey fell backward hard, making a loud thud when his body hit the floor. He stared up at Patrick startled and confused.

He could hear his father choking and gasping as the purple toxins entered his lungs and his bloodstream.

"What the fuck?" Mickey snarled, staring up at Patrick.

Patrick grabbed two rags and rushed to where Mickey lay stunned and disoriented. "Here, use this to cover your face. Don't breathe in any of this shit," Patrick said in a calm and relaxed voice.

Mickey hadn't even thought about protecting himself from the toxins. He had seen his father in trouble and jumped into action. Patrick was always the calm and collected one. The one with a clear head in an emergency.

Clive continued to cough as the purple dust settled to the ground. "What the fuck was that?" Clive choked out.

"Call an ambulance," Patrick ordered Mickey. Patrick covered his face and moved to help Clive off the floor.

"Dad?" Mickey whispered, realizing what had just happened.

Clive shook his head back and forth as if trying to clear the dust from his face. Then his body tightened, and his mouth trembled.

"No, this can't be. What are you doing here?" Clive mumbled, staring at the empty corner in Mickey's office.

Mickey and Patrick looked at each other. There was no one in the corner.

"No! You're dead! This can't be!" Clive grabbed the large glass paperweight Mickey had sitting on his desk and threw it at the empty corner. "Fuck you! Stay away from me!" Clive was shaking and throwing things at the empty space. It was clear that whatever he was seeing had him terrified.

"Pops, it's okay. There's nobody there." Mickey reached for his father and tried to comfort him.

Clive swung around and slashed his son across the arm with the knife he had used to open the box.

Mickey grunted as the knife cut into his flesh.

Patrick lunged at Clive and tackled him to the ground. He wrestled with the frightened man who saw nothing but demons attacking him.

Eventually, Patrick was able to knock the knife out of Clive's hand while Mickey managed to locate a scarf leftover from the winter months and used it to restrain his father.

Clive was sweating profusely and his eyes were bloodshot and dilated. He continued to yell and scream as his invisible attackers continued their assault on his body and mind.

"What the fuck's happening to him?" Mickey whispered, watching this once strong and intimidating man be reduced to shivers and tears. This shit worked so fast.

As the paramedics burst through the office door, Clive's eyes shot open, and he began convulsing.

"Back up, gentlemen, we got him from here," the paramedic commanded, forcing Mickey to move out of the way so he could assess Clive.

"He's going into cardiac arrest!" one of the medics

shouted, reaching into his medic bag.

Mickey and Patrick lurched forward to hold down his father's shoulders while the medics worked on him.

"What's he on?" one of the medics asked.

"We don't know. We think it might be LSD," Patrick responded.

"Since we don't know what's in his system for sure, we can't give him anything."

At that moment, Clive passed out.

The medics lifted Clive onto the stretcher and rushed him to the hospital.

♣ ♣ ♣

The room was quiet except for the steady beeping of the monitors which acted as a constant reminder that his father was hanging on by a thread.

The doctors were running a battery of tests, trying to determine the exact chemicals currently flowing through his father's blood.

The nurses advised that they couldn't give his father any type of medication to ease his suffering until they were certain it would not have an adverse effect with whatever drugs were currently coursing through his veins.

For now, they could only monitor his vitals and wait for the drugs to pass through his system. The doctor was concerned that unless his father was able to relax and reduce his heart rate, he might go into cardiac arrest again.

It appeared that his father was in a constant state of terror, causing his heart rate to spike whenever the hallucinations became too intense.

Mickey had never felt so helpless. All he could do was sit with his father and try to offer him some sort of comfort.

His once strong and intimidating father was now nothing more than a trembling, vulnerable man. Even though he and his father fought all the time, and Mickey hated his father's guts with a passion, in the end, he was still his father. Mickey didn't want to lose the cranky old man.

Mickey turned his head slightly, acknowledging the man standing in the doorway.

"How's he doing?" Patrick asked as he stepped into the room and placed a comforting hand on his best friend's shoulder.

"The tough bastard is hanging in there." Mickey snorted as he turned back to the trembling man.

"He's a strong man. He'll pull through this."

"Any info on who delivered the package?"

"We checked the security footage, and it looks like some woman in a black leather outfit gave Neil the package. She was wearing a motorcycle helmet, so we couldn't get a shot of her face."

"So how do you know that it was a woman?" Mickey asked, watching his father's lip tremble as he stepped into another nightmare.

Patrick smirked behind him. "Cuz of her tits."

Mickey couldn't help but chuckle. "Yeah, guess those would give it away. Keep looking. I need to find this bastard, now."

"Will do. Need anything from me?"

Mickey shook his head as he placed his hand on his father's forearm.

Once Patrick left the room, Mickey's thoughts drifted back to when he was eight years old. Back to the day when he had broken his arm . . .

It was a quiet Saturday morning in August. While most kids were inside eating breakfast and watching cartoons, Mickey was busy sneaking outside to play.

His father had built him a jungle gym in their backyard complete with swings, something that resembled a slide, and a chain link that ran across the top of the structure that he and his friends used to climb across. Out of all the kids, Mickey was the only one to climb the furthest before losing his grip and falling to the ground. He wanted to make his pops proud by showing him how strong he was.

On this particular Saturday, Mickey was feeling bored of the usual backyard activities. Instead, he decided he wanted to go exploring.

The back of their house opened up onto a hill that led down to a ravine. His father had warned him that if he ever caught him playing down by the ravine, he would tear him a new hide.

Normally, Mickey was terrified of his father and would never dream of disobeying his rules. However, on this particular morning, Mickey was angry that his father had refused to come outside and play with him; instead choosing to stay inside and watch the game with his buddy, Joe.

Mickey walked toward the edge of the yard and glanced over his shoulder to make sure no one was watching. Realizing the coast was clear, he began to slowly make his way down the rocky embankment.

It had rained the last two nights, so the ground was muddy and slippery. Mickey carefully stepped onto one of the large boulders that stuck out of the dirt and stared at the ravine below. He felt like Columbus discovering America. No one was going to tell him what to do. He was a big boy.

At that very moment, the earth beneath the rock shifted under Mickey's weight and the boulder came loose from its position. Mickey let out a scream as he fell from the rock and tumbled the rest of the way down the hill until he landed at the edge of the ravine.

Mickey cried out in pain as he lay covered in blood and mud. His body hit several rocks and jagged edges cutting deep into his flesh as he fell down the embankment.

He felt a shooting pain in his left arm and let out a horrid cry when he realized that his arm was resting at an unnatural angle.

Mickey continued to cry and shout for help, fearing that

no one would find him. Tears streamed down his face as he imagined never being found and never seeing his father again.

The creative imagination of a child began to run wild as he imagined the most horrible, gruesome ends to his life. What if a wolf found him? Or a bear? Did trolls exist in the ravines of Jersey?

The injured and scared little boy cried out for his father once again, praying he would hear his shouts and come to his aid.

A few minutes later, among his cries, Mickey heard the sound of his father's worried voice calling down to him.

"He's down here! Joe, call an ambulance!" his father hollered as he made his way down the slippery slope.

Mickey had never heard such fear or panic in his father's voice before. He had been frightened that when his father found him, he would be furious and would beat him. But instead, when his father finally reached him, he scooped him up in his arms and hugged him tightly. His father carefully carried him up the hill, holding him firmly against his chest as if someone might snatch him from his arms.

"Everything is gonna be all right, son. Poppa's got ya. You're gonna be just fine, little man," his father choked out.

Mickey couldn't stop the tears from rolling down his face. He was in so much pain, but the sound of his father's worried voice somehow soothed him. His father wasn't mad. His father was scared. Scared for him.

That was the moment Mickey realized that behind that angry, mean facade hid a loving father who cared deeply about his son.

After that day, his father never showed such emotions again. But Mickey knew they were there . . . buried deep beneath the rubble.

Mickey held his father's hand and wiped away the tear that slid down his cheek.

Hang in there, Pops. Mickey's got ya now.

CHAPTER 21- Seth

Seth rubbed his eyes for the second time in the past ten minutes. He had been staring at crime scene photos and reading his notes for the past three hours trying to identify any clue, any link, anything that might help point them in the right direction.

So far, all he'd managed to do was give himself a headache. His eyes were dry and he needed a break.

He jumped at the sound of someone knocking at his door.

Seth glanced at his cell phone. It was just after 9 PM. He hoped it wasn't Mickey trying to apologize once again.

Although, if it wasn't him, who else could it be at this late hour?

Oh, great. Here was the part where he got raped and

murdered. Just another night in Jersey.

Maybe he should invest in a gun?

Seth stood behind his door, wondering what good it was having a peephole when an intruder could easily just shoot him in the eye once he looked through the hole. Doesn't seem very safe when you think about it.

He held his breath as he peeked through the hole, hoping not to see the image of the man who wanted to murder him.

"Oh!" Seth said, surprised and a bit relieved when he recognized the man standing on the other side.

On second thought, he wasn't sure how safe he really was.

"You know, I could've easily shot you in the face when you peeked through the hole," Patrick said once Seth opened the door. "Plus, you walk heavy. Could hear ya approaching the door a mile away." Patrick didn't wait for an invitation. He stepped past Seth and walked on in.

"Good to see you, too." Seth closed the door and followed Patrick into the living room.

"Nice piece of shit you got here. Reminds me of the first place Mickey and I shared when we were younger."

"Did you just come here to insult me? Or did you need something?" Seth was feeling agitated. Plus, he wasn't totally comfortable being alone in his apartment with the gang's torturer. Something about that just screamed *danger*.

Patrick turned and stared at Seth. His emerald eyes caught Seth off guard. They were the same shade as Mickey's. Patrick looked unsure for a moment but then decided to go ahead.

"Look. I know you and Mickey have this thing going between you two. And I know something happened about a week ago because he has been a right miserable bastard ever since."

Seth opened his mouth to protest, but Patrick raised his hand to silence him.

"I know Mickey better than anyone, so I know when he is crazy in love with someone. Actually, this is the first time I have ever seen the bastard in love. So, that tells me you are special. Somehow you broke through that concrete he has wrapped around his heart. And because of that, I know you're good for him. You are what he needs.

"Which brings me to why I'm here. Mickey's father was attacked this morning and is currently in the hospital, probably about to die."

Seth gasped, bringing his hands up to cover the shock on his face.

"Mickey will probably kick my ass for coming here, but I don't care. He's my brother, and he's in pain. He needs you. So, whatever this fight thing is about, suck it up, and get your ass to the hospital. Now."

Seth shook his head quickly and grabbed his keys off the kitchen counter. His heart was pounding in his chest, but Mickey needed him.

Patrick explained what had happened to Clive on the drive to the hospital. At this point, they were hoping the drugs would burn through his system before his heart gave out. Apparently, he had already had two mild heart attacks since breathing in the toxins. Whatever was in that drug was potent and worked fast.

"Mickey didn't want anyone to know about us," Seth finally confessed, breaking the long silence in the car.

Patrick glanced at Seth with sympathetic eyes.

"Please keep this to yourself. I'll be there for Mickey to help him get through this, but I can't be with someone who is afraid to be themselves. I can't go through my life feeling like someone's dirty little secret." Seth stared at his hands as he confessed his true feelings. "That was what the fight was about. I pulled away when he rejected me in front of his friends."

Patrick reached over and took Seth's hand.

Seth flinched at first, suspicious of his touch, but relaxed when he realized Patrick was simply trying to connect with him on an emotional level.

"I know you don't know me, and you have no reason to trust a thing I say. But deep down Mickey is a good guy. Yes, he has a rough exterior and doesn't lead the most law-abiding life, but that's because he was born into this life. His father is the boss. Mickey was never given a choice about his future. His father has been grooming him to take over the family once he steps aside. This is all he knows."

"The family?" Seth asked.

"As you get to know us more, you'll realize we are more like a big, extended family. We look out for each other; take care of one another. We even look out for the community. If you look past all the bullshit and machoism, you will see the kind dude who plays football with kids on Sundays, checks in on the elderly woman who runs the bakery at the end of the street, and even donates a quarter of his legitimate salary to the woman's shelter down the block.

"Someone like Mickey deserves to be happy and deserves to be with the person who makes him happy. I know it might be tough, but if you're interested in seeing where things go with Mickey, you guys got my support." Patrick squeezed Seth's hand briefly before returning it to the wheel.

Seth couldn't believe the support coming from Patrick. For someone who got off on breaking people's bones, he was quite sensitive.

"Thanks, Patrick. That means a lot coming from you."

Patrick smirked. "Plus, if anyone says anything to you guys or gives you any shit, just send them my way and I'll take care of them like I did Brody."

Seth laughed. Patrick was a good guy when you got to know him.

"Can I ask, when did you first suspect something was going on? I thought we were being discreet."

"I knew the moment he called me off. Mickey has never gotten in the way of me doing my thing. But the way he acted when he saw you tied to that chair, and the way he protected you from me, that was when I knew something was going on. Mickey has never been that protective over anyone before."

Seth turned to face the window and discreetly smiled. He could feel his insides warm.

They arrived at the hospital ten minutes later. The true challenge was trying to sneak past the head nurse, Nurse May who had eyes like a hawk.

"Man, I hate that woman," Patrick whispered. "She already busted me for sneaking outside food into the hospital so that Mickey could eat something that doesn't taste like sweaty ass." Seth let out a tiny chuckle. "Then I try and get Mickey a more comfortable chair, and she pushes me out of the way and says 'This ain't the Ritz! You ain't here for luxury!' That's all before she called me a skinny twig and waddled off. Have you seen these muscles?" Patrick flexed his bicep clearly fishing for a compliment. Seth just rolled his eyes.

"So, how do we gat past her?" Seth asked, peeking around the wall.

"The only way to get past this woman's defenses is to throw her off her game. This means distraction. Unfortunately flirting won't work on this woman. Something tells me that she would rather sit on my face and suffocate me, then get on her knees and suck my dick. I got an idea."

Patrick slipped past the nurse's station and started

playing with the pamphlets that hung on the wall. He pretended to read one on herpes and then put it back in with the pamphlets for gonorrhea.

Nurse May clenched her teeth watching him.

Next, Patrick bent down and grabbed a handful of free condoms, and shoved them into his pocket. He smiled at Nurse May as he spun back around to look at the Pamphlets. This time, his arm hit the display, causing the whole thing to crash to the floor. Pamphlets and condoms were scattered across the hallway.

"What the . . . ?" Nurse May cursed as she jumped from her chair and stomped toward Patrick.

Seth chuckled and slipped past Nurse May while her back was turned. He heard Patrick cry out in pain as she grabbed him by the ear and proceeded to drag him down the hallway.

"Good luck, buddy," Seth whispered sympathetically as he slipped into Clive's room.

Seth's heart stopped in his chest when his eyes fell on Mickey. Mickey was sitting next to his father's bed holding his arm while his father's body thrashed around on the bed.

Mickey looked up as Seth walked in. It broke Seth's heart seeing the worry in Mickey's eyes.

"What are you doing here?" Mickey choked, surprised to see him.

"Patrick told me about your father. How's he doing?" Seth placed a hand on Mickey's shoulder hoping to provide some form of comfort.

Mickey looked back at his father. "He's been like this for hours. He's hallucinating, living through an endless nightmare. It's not clear what he's seein' or if he even knows I'm here. The nurses had to restrain him so he wouldn't hurt himself or anyone else."

Seth noticed the thick leather straps fastened around Clive's wrists and ankles. It couldn't be comfortable wearing those things. "When will it stop?"

"Doctors don't know. They're worried that if his heart rate doesn't go down, he'll go into cardiac arrest."

"Can't they give him anything to reduce his heart rate or knock him out?" Seth asked as he gazed at all the equipment surrounding Clive's bed.

"They can't take the risk. Since they don't know what was in the drug, they're worried the drugs might react to each other. Right now, we just have to wait for them to work their way through his system."

Seth rubbed Mickey's shoulder. "I hope it's okay that I'm here. I know this must be tough for you."

Mickey gazed up at Seth with such grateful eyes. "You don't know what it means having you here." Mickey grabbed Seth's hand and gave it a gentle squeeze.

Seth's heart filled with warmth at his touch. His hands were big and rough. They were the hands of someone who had worked hard their entire life.

"I'm here for you. Whatever you need. How about I go

grab us a coffee? I saw a machine just down the hall." Seth pointed over his shoulder.

"Yeah, that would be great. Thanks, babe." Mickey attempted to give Seth a smile, but his pain showed through resulting in a wary grimace.

"I'll be right back." Seth walked out into the hallway being sure to remain hidden from Nurse May's watchful eye.

Seth was glad the machine was in working order and moved quickly to get their coffees. He was carrying the coffees back to Clive's room when the sound of alarms screeching made him jump.

He watched in horror as several nurses rushed into Clive's room. A moment later, he heard Mickey's voice pleading for his father to hang on and not to give up.

Seth stood frozen in the hallway. His feet wouldn't move no matter how much he begged them to.

Shouts were heard as nurses rushed to move equipment around the room and perform checks. Seth finally found his strength and stepped into the room.

Mickey was standing against the wall, watching helplessly as nurses and a doctor did what they could to assist Clive. Clive's body was shaking on the bed as his skin turned pale white.

Seth dropped the coffees into the trash by the door and rushed to Mickey's side. He slid his hand into Mickey's and squeezed, hoping he could transfer his courage and support into Mickey's stunned body.

He wasn't sure if Mickey was even aware of his presence. He stood there, motionless, watching the chaos unfold in the room.

The alarms continued blaring, until one sound cut through all the rest. The sound of the heart rate monitor flat-lining.

Seth's heart dropped when he heard Mickey whisper one gut-wrenching word . . .

"Dad . . ."

CHAPTER 22 - Seth

It was shortly after midnight when they left the hospital. Patrick and Seth helped an unresponsive Mickey into the backseat of Patrick's Porsche. Mickey remained silent as he stared absently out the side window.

Seth wondered what was going through Mickey's head. Was he reliving a memory with his father? Was he questioning god's plan? Or was he busy plotting revenge? Any would be reasonable given the shock of his father's death.

"Do you think he'll be all right?" Seth asked Patrick, eyes still glued on Mickey in the backseat.

Patrick glanced at his friend in the rearview mirror. "Give it some time. This is how he processes his emotions. Don't be surprised if he spaces out and doesn't say much to you for a few days."

Seth wasn't sure if he could handle the distance. All he

wanted to do was hold Mickey in his arms and tell him everything was going to be all right. It hurt him to see Mickey in so much pain and there was nothing he could do about it.

That's not true . . . he could find the bastard behind these murders and make them suffer. The thought of getting revenge for Mickey made Seth want to smile.

Patrick drove them to Mickey's penthouse condo located in a trendy up-and-coming area of Jersey's downtown core.

Seth's eyes widened when Patrick opened the door to the two-bedroom condo overlooking the city. The living room was sleek and modern, not exactly what you would have expected from a guy who owned a strip club, bar, and was heir to the criminal underworld of Jersey.

The living room had two large, leather couches facing each other—perfect for conversing with company. In the center of the room was a glass fireplace separating the living room from what appeared to be a large social gaming area.

The gaming room was every man-child's wet dream. In the center sat a large pool table waiting for its next challenger to rack up the balls. Off to the side was a decent-sized poker table with red and black poker chips stacked neatly.

Finally, against the farthest wall sat a large entertainment center complete with a sixty-inch flat screen, a couple of lazy boy massage chairs, and an expensive-looking stereo system.

Seth's mouth dropped open at the sight of Mickey's amazing home. He didn't want to venture a guess as to how much this place must have cost. Apparently, crime did pay. Very well.

Past the living room, the penthouse opened up to a large black-and-white marble kitchen. The high-end stainless-steel appliances added to the seemingly expensive taste of one, Mr. O'Brien.

It appeared Mickey had great taste when it came to all things. Or did he just know a lot of clumsy delivery men? Perhaps he learned a thing or two from the Italians.

"Do you want to rest here, or in the bedroom, buddy?" Patrick asked, nodding toward the living room.

Mickey walked to the couch without responding and flopped down.

"He'll be fine. Just needs some time," Patrick tried to reassure Seth. "Do you want me to give you a lift home or are you gonna stay the night?"

"I'll stay here. I want to be here for him in case he needs anything." Seth wrapped his arms around his chest not sure what to do with himself.

Patrick nodded his head. "That's just what he needs. I'll come check on you guys in the morning. There's food in the fridge, and I'm sure you already know where the bedroom is."

Patrick's grin faded when Seth shook his head.

"Guess you guys haven't gotten to that part of the relationship yet."

"Not yet. Just met at my place so far."

"Well, the bedroom's down the hall. One with the king bed. Bathroom is to the left."

"Thanks, Patrick. I appreciate everything you've done tonight." Seth brushed his hand gently along Patrick's arm.

"Yeah, well, who doesn't love getting up close and intimate with an angry nurse." Patrick winked at Seth. "Oh, yeah. Got these pics off the security cams at the club today from when Clive was attacked. You can add them to your case file." Patrick tossed an envelope on the marble countertop.

"Thanks. I'll take a look a bit later. Going to get this guy all settled in first."

Seth walked Patrick to the door and thanked him once again. Closing the door, Seth made his way back into the living room to check on Mickey.

Mickey was standing at the balcony window, staring out into the darkness. His eyes were vacant, appearing to be caught in some distant memory.

The view was gorgeous. So many lights flickering in the darkness across from *"the city that never sleeps."* It was so peaceful.

Seth hoped the view would calm Mickey and help him process his loss. He couldn't imagine losing a parent. Yes, he was not currently speaking to his, but he didn't wish them any ill will. He would still be devastated if either of them passed away. Family was family. You loved them unconditionally, even if they broke your heart and turned their backs on you.

Seth placed his hand gently on Mickey's shoulder. "How about I make you something to eat. I'm sure you didn't have much all day."

Mickey placed his hand on top of Seth's and nodded slightly. At least he knew Seth was there.

Seth turned and was about to make his way to the kitchen when he heard Mickey whisper, "Thanks." It was so soft, but Seth had heard it and smiled.

Once in the kitchen, he rummaged through the fridge and pantry, trying to decide what to make for someone who had just experienced extreme loss. It should probably be some sort of comfort food.

Finally, he settled on making a nice veggie omelet with a side of toast with strawberry jam. Keeping it light and healthy would be good to soothe Mickey's late-night hunger. It wasn't much, but Seth hoped the small gesture might help comfort Mickey and show him that he had people around him who cared.

Seth picked up the plate of food and made his way back into the living room.

Mickey stood in the dark room, staring at a picture he had on the far mantle. It appeared to be a picture of him and his father sharing a pint of beer. Both had huge smiles plastered on their faces as if they had both just won the lottery.

"I made you . . . " Seth began but was cut short when he noticed the dark figure sneaking up behind Mickey. Mickey had his back turned and was unaware of their presence. "Mickey watch out!" Seth shouted as he instinctively leaped toward the figure.

The figure was startled by Seth's sudden appearance and quickly turned away from Mickey and toward Seth.

Mickey stumbled to the floor, startled by the sudden commotion.

Seth's movements were too slow.

The figure spun around and blew a hand full of Purple Dust directly into Seth's face before his body slammed into the figure.

Stunned, Seth began coughing and choking as he breathed in the toxic particles. Each new cough sent mouthfuls of dust down his throat and into his lungs. He couldn't catch his breath. All he could taste were chemicals as he unintentionally continued to swallow the toxins. The shit was everywhere.

His lungs burned and his head began to swim. He felt someone push him over, then realized he had landed on the attacker.

He heard Mickey shout and the sound of something large crash and break. Seth rolled on the ground as he struggled to breathe and catch his breath. No fresh oxygen would enter his lungs. He was suffocating.

Seth caught a glimpse of Mickey fighting someone dressed all in black. He needed to help Mickey but was too disoriented. He placed his hand on the floor and tried to push himself up to his feet, but the world around him continued to move.

Another crash was heard as Mickey threw the figure's body against a large painting that hung on the wall.

Seth was almost to his feet, trying to steady the shakiness in his legs. "Mickey . . . " Seth gasped, still struggling to breathe.

He watched as colors and lights flashed before his eyes. The room began to dim, then suddenly became bright. He closed his eyes as flash after flash of exploding color and light assaulted his vision.

Sound around him was beginning to change, moving from a silent whisper to a sudden burst of sound.

Seth's eyes fell on Mickey, who was still fighting their attacker. His head felt like it was going to explode. His body swayed as he tried to straighten himself.

Slowly, Seth's eyes shifted across the living room and stopped in horror when they landed on another figure standing in the hallway leading toward the bedroom.

The man just stood there, staring at Seth. Seth could only make out the shape of the man, he could not focus on any details of his face.

Colors continued to dance in front of Seth's eyes as he tried to focus on the mysterious man in the hallway. He blinked and suddenly the figure was gone.

The hallway was empty.

"Mickey . . . ?" Seth's voice was soft and shallow. His head swam as the floor beneath his feet began to shift. "I . . . can't . . ."

Seth glanced at Mickey once again. His eyes landed on the dark figure that was suddenly charging toward him. As the figure approached, Seth watched as their dark face morphed, shimmered, then came into focus.

Seth let out a horrifying scream as the bloodied face of a man with empty eye sockets came charging at him.

"Seth, watch out!" Mickey shouted from the floor.

But it was too late.

Seth felt something cold and hard connect with the side of his head and everything around him suddenly went dark.

Vision slowly returned. Darkened shapes began to take form. The room was dark and still. The only light to cut through the eerie stillness streamed in through a dirty old window.

Seth's gaze drifted across the room. Where was he? He was lying in a bed, but the room looked unfamiliar.

He scanned the space, hoping to locate something, anything familiar that could tell him where he was. The comforter draped across his body was old and ripped and smelled like it had been sitting in mold for ages.

Beside the bed was a large wooden bureau with three of the nobs missing from its drawers. Somehow, there was mud and leaves crumpled against the surface of the mirror and dresser, adding to the deteriorating condition of the once beautiful piece of furniture.

Seth could feel the panic beginning to build. Where was he? What had happened? Whose bed was he in?

His breath began to quicken.

This was what happened when you hooked up with strange men on Grindr. You woke up chained to their bed in their creepy, dirty, old house.

Fuck. He had to get out of here.

Seth's breath caught in his chest as he heard one of the floorboards squeak.

His eyes darted toward the bedroom door.

Standing in the doorframe was a young boy, no older than six. His clothes were dirty and ripped around the edges with dark-colored stains splattered across his chest. Was that blood?

In the boy's left hand a scorched teddy bear dangled missing one of its arms.

The boy stood motionless in the doorway facing Seth. There was something eerie about this kid. Something not quite right . . .

"Are you okay?" Seth whispered too terrified to move.

Silence.

Seth blinked and when he opened his eyes, the boy stood inside the room a few feet from the door. Seth jerked in bed, startled by the boy's sudden movement.

"What the fuck?" Seth gasped, staring at the boy who remained silent and motionless. "Who are . . ." Seth's voice caught in his throat as he noticed the boy was missing the left part of his head.

Where the boy's skull should have been was an empty space oozing black fluid.

"What the fuck?" Seth cried out as his heart raced.

The boy remained still, staring at Seth with his vacant, dead eyes.

Seth glanced around the room, searching for an escape. He let out another scream when he turned back to the boy, only to find him now standing at the foot of his bed.

Black liquid continued to ooze down the side of the boy's open skull, slowly dripping onto the tattered material of his shirt. What the hell happened to this kid?

Seth's heart continued to race as the terrifying image before him took hold.

This couldn't be real. The boy couldn't be real. He was losing his mind. He was fast asleep somewhere having a nightmare. It had to be.

Seth covered his eyes and closed them tight. "You're not real! You're not real!" Seth shouted as the pounding in his chest continued to increase.

This had to be a dream. He would wake up in his own bed, safe and sound. He'd probably drank too much and passed out reading that freakin' Stephen King book. There was no way this could be real.

He refused to open his eyes. He knew that this had to be a dream. He would wake up any moment now . . . Any moment . . .

Seth felt the mattress beneath him shift and he began to cry. "You're not real! This is just a dream!" He felt another shift, this time moving closer to his midsection.

The boy was crawling on the bed. The shifting of the mattress was him moving closer. Don't open your eyes . . . He's right there . . . He could feel the chill of the boy's body against his . . .

The mattress shifted once more, causing Seth's shoulders to sink into the mattress. He refused to open his eyes. He didn't want to see the boy's dead eyes staring down at him.

He could smell the rot.

Then . . . he felt the boy's breath against his neck.

Seth let out a horrified scream. "Please! You're not real! Somebody help!"

Seth couldn't move his body. He wanted to get up and run, but his limbs would not cooperate.

The boy's breath grew warmer as his body leaned closer to Seth's face.

Seth was in tears. This was it. He was going to die. "Please! Somebody help me! I don't want to die!"

Seth felt so alone, helpless, and terrified. No one was coming for him. No one cared. There was no one to protect him. This was it. He was all alone in this room of horrors, waiting for his end. And no one cared.

Seth continued to cry.

How come no one loved him?

Because he was a loser, and no one cared.

"Please . . . I don't want to die," Seth whispered as another tear slid down his cheek.

No one was coming . . .

He was alone . . .

This was his end . . .

Seth could feel his clenched eyes loosening. He wanted this nightmare to end. He just needed to gaze into the boy's dead eyes and let him take him . . . . Then he would be at peace.

"Hold on for me, babe!" the words were soft and distant. Barely audible.

What? What was that?

The mattress shifted once again as the dead boy inched closer. "Please, don't hurt me . . . I don't want to die . . . " Seth pleaded, knowing it was pointless.

"Hang in there, Seth! Please! I'm right here with you,

buddy!" the voice was distant and sounded vaguely familiar.

Where had he heard that voice before? Was someone here to rescue him?

"Please. Somebody help me!" He hoped that someone would hear him. Perhaps there was hope.

Seth screamed once again as he felt the boy's firm grip on his arm. This was it. The boy had him now.

"You're not alone, babe. I'm right here with you. Concentrate on my voice. It's me, Mickey."

Mickey? Who . . . Why does that name sound so familiar?

More breathing against Seth's neck as the grip on his arm tightened.

"Please . . . I love you . . . "

Suddenly the flood gates of recognition burst open.

Mickey. His Mickey. He wasn't alone. Mickey was here to save him.

"Mickey? Please, help me!" Seth tried to shout, but his voice felt deep.

"You can do this. It's not real. Whatever you're seeing. It's just a nightmare. Nothing can hurt you," Mickey's voice was becoming louder as his words penetrated the fog in his mind.

Seth could still feel the boy's breath on his neck, but

his grip was beginning to loosen.

"Please, hold on for me, babe. I can't lose you. Concentrate on my voice. I need you to hold on for me. Whatever you're seeing isn't real. You're safe in my arms, here with me in my bed. Please, Seth. Hang on for me. I can't lose you too."

Mickey's words filled Seth's heart. He wasn't alone. Mickey was here with him. Holding him tight in his arms. He was . . . loved . . .

Seth felt another tear slide down his cheek, but this time the tear was not shed out of fear . . . but out of love. He wasn't alone. Someone needed him. Someone loved him. He needed to hold on.

Slowly Seth felt the mattress shift beneath his body once again, but this time it seemed the boy was retreating . . . moving back toward the foot of the bed.

Seth's heartbeat was beginning to slow down. He just needed to hold on.

"I'm here with you, babe. God, I love you."

Seth swore he could feel Mickey's lips press gently against his right cheek. Perhaps it was real. Perhaps it was all in his head. Either way, Seth began to relax and for the first time, feel safe.

"I'm here, Mickey. I can feel you." Seth smiled, keeping his eyes closed while he concentrated on the sweet sound of his savior's voice.

Mickey.

His Mickey. The man who kept him safe.

CHAPTER 23 - Mickey

Mickey lay on the floor, head throbbing. His attacker had hit him with something solid. He hadn't seen what it was. Only felt the impact, then felt the floor give way beneath him.

He shook his head, trying to clear the fog from his mind and ringing in his ears. Fuck. He couldn't wait. He needed to get up and end this piece of shit.

The world swayed for a moment as he turned onto his side. The figure in black was charging toward Seth, who was still coughing and gasping for air. Mickey's eyes fell on the ceramic object still dangling from his attacker's hand.

Panic set in as he realized that Seth was directly in the path of his attacker's escape.

"Seth, watch out!" Mickey shouted from the floor, but it was too late.

Mickey watched in horror as the ceramic leprechaun connected with Seth's head with such force that Seth's body went flying backward, crashing into one of the end tables before slumping over on the floor.

"Seth!" Mickey screamed as he jumped to his feet and rushed to his side.

Mickey ignored the figure in black as they rushed out onto the balcony and disappear over the ledge.

Mickey pulled Seth's body against his and quickly listened to see if Seth was breathing. He was, but barely.

Thank God he was still alive.

Mickey quickly felt for a pulse. It was strong. Good. That was a good sign.

Next, Mickey quickly ran his hands across Seth's body, feeling for any blood or broken bones. Other than the blood trickling down from where Seth was hit in the head, the rest of him seemed okay.

Now what? Should he take him to the hospital?

For what? So he can sit and watch him at the side of a hospital bed?

No. He had to find a way to keep Seth calm. The doctor said the drug made people hallucinate. It kept the person in such a heightened state of terror that their heart eventually gave up.

No. There was no way he was going to let Seth die as well. No way.

He scooped Seth up and carried him into his bedroom. Seth groaned softly as his face twisted. Perhaps he was having a nightmare? At least he was still alive and breathing. That had to be a good sign.

Mickey flopped down on the bed with his back against the headboard. He pulled Seth's body up against his and wrapped his arms protectively around Seth's torso.

"Please, Seth, hold on. Don't leave me," Mickey heard himself say as he gently rocked Seth back and forth.

He brushed some of the matted, bloody hair from Seth's delicate face. He looked like an angel sleeping in his arms. So quiet and peaceful. He looked so innocent.

"I'm here with you, buddy. Please don't leave me." Mickey held Seth's body tight against his chest.

He could feel Seth's body temperature rise. His lips parted and he let out a small groan as though he were uncomfortable. Mickey watched as Seth's eyebrows turned inward and his face contorted as though he were struggling against something. It was clear that Seth was having a nightmare.

Beads of sweat formed on Seth's forehead while his body jerked from side to side. Seth was fighting against something in his dream.

"No!" Seth cried out. "You're not real! You're not real!"

Startled, Mickey held onto Seth's body even tighter as he thrashed around, trying to claw his way free from

Mickey, free from his nightmare. Whatever Seth was seeing in his dream was terrifying the poor guy.

Mickey didn't know what to do. His heart broke watching Seth's sweet and gentle face contort in fear and pain. He wanted to make it stop; take away all of Seth's pain and torment.

He held him close to his chest as Seth screamed out in terror.

What happened if he couldn't get Seth to calm down? What happened if his fear kept escalating until his heart finally gave up like his father's? He couldn't lose two people he cared about in the same night.

Fuck. Seth was never supposed to be here. If he had just stayed clear of Seth's life and not followed him out of the bar that night, Seth would not be suffering right now. Seth was here because he was taking care of him.

Seth with his kind heart and gentle soul.

This was what Mickey got for living the life he had. He had caused so much pain and misery in so many lives; this was karma exacting her revenge on him. Making him pay for all his sins.

He was a monster and deserved to suffer.

"Please, don't take him from me. Seth is innocent. He doesn't deserve any of this. He doesn't deserve to be punished for my sins." Mickey kissed the top of Seth's head as a tear rolled down his cheek.

Why had he wasted so much time fighting against his

feelings for Seth? Now, he may never get the chance to see his smiling face again. Hear him laugh. Watch him roll his eyes whenever Mickey said something stupid or immature.

Seth let out another cry of pain. Mickey watched as tears began to slide down Seth's cheeks. He could feel his heart pounding. Whatever he was seeing, he was terrified.

He felt so powerless. He had promised to protect him. Yet here he was, failing him once again.

He needed Seth to know he was here for him. That he was safe in his arms.

"Hang in there, Seth! Please! I'm right here with you, buddy!" Mickey shouted in frustration.

Mickey's breath caught in his chest. He swore he saw Seth's head jerk toward his voice.

Had he heard him?

"You're not alone, babe. I'm right here with you. Concentrate on my voice. It's me, Mickey," Mickey spoke into Seth's ear, hoping he could hear his voice.

This time he felt Seth breathe in quickly as if he recognized his voice. Mickey felt a giant weight lift off his chest. There was hope. If he could get Seth to concentrate on his voice, perhaps he could calm him down. Calm him enough to bring down his heart rate and keep him relaxed until the drugs passed through his system. He needed to try.

"You can do this. It's not real. Whatever you're seeing. It's just a nightmare. Nothing can hurt ya."

Seth's body was still tense, but Mickey could feel his muscles relaxing slightly. It was progress. He could do this.

Mickey squeezed Seth tight and kissed his cheek. He loved this guy so fucking much. Why did it take almost losing him to realize how much Seth meant to him?

If Seth survived this, Mickey was going to spend the rest of his life worshiping the man. Giving him everything he could ever want and always protecting him. No pain would ever come to him again. His heart belonged to this sweet man.

Mickey spent the next few hours talking into Seth's ear, holding him tight, kissing his head, doing whatever he could to make Seth feel safe and loved while he was trapped in his living nightmare.

The sun was beginning to crack through the bedroom blinds when Mickey felt Seth's body shift in his arms. Mickey's face was resting cheek to cheek with Seth's as he spoke to him gently.

"Mickey . . . ?" his voice was soft and groggy.

Mickey's eyes shot open. "Seth? Baby! You're awake!" Mickey threw his huge arms around Seth and buried him in a tight bear hug. He couldn't believe Seth was awake. Seth had survived.

Seth's words were strained as his lungs were being squished by Mickey's powerful arms. "Hey, stud. It's good to see you, too, but you're cutting off my airway."

"Oh, shit! Sorry." Mickey relaxed his hold but refused

to let Seth out of his arms. He showered him with kisses.

A feeling of relief washed over Mickey as he silently thanked the gods for giving him this miracle.

Seth giggled in Mickey's arms. "I could hear you. Your voice."

"What?" Mickey asked, too focused on never letting his boy go, ever again.

"You're voice. I heard it in my dream. It was the only thing that calmed me down."

"I couldn't lose you," Mickey said as he leaned in for yet another kiss on Seth's cheek.

"That nightmare, it felt so real. I was convinced I was going to die. But then I heard your voice. At first, it was distant, but then it got closer, and I began feeling warmth all around me. It's strange, but at that moment, I suddenly felt safe. I *knew* I was safe . . . Safe in your arms, and you weren't going to let anything bad happen to me."

"And I never will. I will always be here for you. Protecting you with my dying breath." Mickey leaned forward and kissed Seth's dry lips.

Seth pulled away and locked eyes with Mickey's. "Just so you know, I love you, too." Seth smiled at Mickey, making him fall in love with him all over again.

Mickey wondered if Seth had heard him say "I love you" while unconscious. Apparently, he had.

"Hearing you say those words—that was the turning

point that saved me. I could feel the love. I needed to survive so I could tell you I love you too." Seth rolled and straddled Mickey's lap. "Thank you for loving me. You saved my life." Seth gazed into Mickey's emerald eyes.

Mickey pulled Seth's body close and kissed him passionately. He was never going to let this man go. His heart belonged to him.

CHAPTER 24- Seth

Seth fell back asleep and slept for another few hours. His body and mind were exhausted from the ordeal he had gone through. When he finally woke, he was starving and dying of thirst.

Seth's bare feet were silent as they moved along the wood floors toward the living room. He could hear voices speaking and wondered if he should hang back and stay out of sight. Perhaps Mickey would get mad if he was seen in his apartment.

Then he recognized the voice. Patrick.

Patrick and Mickey stopped talking once Seth appeared in the hallway.

"You're awake!" Mickey walked toward Seth and wrapped his arms around him. There was no point in pretending. Patrick knew they were fucking.

"How are ya feelin'?" Patrick asked from the couch. He sat with his leg resting on his knee and his arm on the top of the couch. Clearly, comfortable where he was.

Mickey guided Seth to the couch and then pulled him down onto his lap, wrapping his arms around his body.

The feel of Mickey's muscular arms wrapped around him sent a wave of warmth throughout his system. How could one man's touch feel so good?

"My head is a bit sore, and I'm dying of thirst."

"Here drink this." Mickey passed him a cold bottle of water that had been sitting on the end table next to him.

"You sure?" Seth didn't want to steal Mickey's water.

"Anything mine is yours, babe." Mickey gave him a wink that would have caused his panties to drop had Patrick not been in the room. Damn.

Seth opened the bottle and chugged. The cold liquid felt so refreshing traveling down Seth's parched throat. How was it possible for water to taste so damn good?

"I'm sorry I wasn't here for you guys," Patrick started, leaning forward with a concerned look on his face. "I'm getting security to make me copies of their surveillance footage, so hopefully we can get some sort of clue as to who this bastard is. Looks like they came in through the balcony. Must be an expert climber."

"Judging by the photos I've seen they look like they are in pretty decent shape." Seth placed the cap back on the bottle and spotted an envelope on the table. "Are those the pics from yesterday at the club?" Seth asked Patrick, pointing at the envelope.

"Yeah. Brought them here last night for you to add to your creeper collection. Guess you haven't checked 'em out yet." Patrick tucked a stray blue hair that had fallen loose back behind his ear.

Even though the guy was covered in tattoos with a crazy hairstyle, he still managed to look like a rough, hot supermodel. He probably had a revolving door at his place as well. There was something about a hot, muscular, tattooed Irish guy that always made people drop to their knees.

Seth picked up the envelope, then laid back against his man's chest. Mickey slid his hand up and down his thigh, causing Seth's pants to tighten.

He glanced up at Patrick and blushed. Patrick had evidently seen the sudden rise in Seth's pants which was made clear by his little smirk.

Mickey rested his chin on Seth's shoulder and whispered into his ear, "Don't forget who you belong to."

Seth turned to face Mickey, shocked that he would even suggest he was into his friend. "When I'm in a relationship, I'm a one dick kind of guy."

"Is that what we are? In a relationship?" Mickey asked with a wicked smile.

Seth went silent.

Mickey's body tensed as he watched his face

expectantly. "What? You telling me that you don't want to date me? What was all that about in the bedroom?"

"Wow! I really don't need to be hearing any of this, guys." Patrick threw up both hands.

Seth shot Patrick a death stare. "It's not like that." He turned to face Mickey. "Look, I love you, and I know you love me."

"So, what's the problem?" Mickey looked confused.

"The problem is, I realized the other night at Coney Island that it can never work between us."

Mickey's mouth fell open. "What do you mean?"

"I mean, I don't want to be in a relationship in which I have to hide. The other day you introduced me as the 'guy working with Paddy.' You didn't even acknowledge me as a friend.

"I don't want to be the mistress waiting in the shadows, hoping her man will stop by and show her a bit of love and attention. I want to be the guy holding your hand as you introduce me as your boyfriend, laying claim to me as your own." Seth's eyes fell to his hands.

Mickey could see the hurt and pain in Seth's face. It wasn't fair to hide such a bright gem under a veil of secrecy. Such beauty deserved to be on display. Deserved to be acknowledged and worshiped.

"I would never ask you to come out when you're not ready. I'm just saying that my heart can't handle being pushed aside. So, it may be better if we were just . . .

friends." Seth placed his hand on top of Mickey's heart and stared at his hand.

Mickey's heart was beating fast with the prospect of losing him. He glanced at Patrick, who gave him a look that said he was being an idiot.

"I know it's none of my business and this is between you guys. But, Mickey, *what the fuck* is wrong with you?"

Patrick's comment caught Mickey off guard. He was not expecting that.

"Your bastard of an old man is dead. You're now the leader of the crew. Do you think anyone in their right mind would dare say a thing about who you fuck? Sorry—who you're dating?"

Patrick had a point. His fear had mostly been of his father and his old-fashioned contempt for homos and their "fag life."

"You're a badass mother fucker. If anyone has a problem with you swallowing dick, then they will have to deal with your fists."

Mickey smirked at the thought of breaking any guy's nose who had a problem with him and Seth being together. To be honest . . . with his father's passing, things had now changed.

He no longer had someone to be accountable to. He was the big boss now. People were accountable to him. That also meant everything now fell on his shoulders. He was responsible for the family, their business, even making sure the community was safe.

It was a new age.

Mickey gently caressed Seth's face, turning it so he could gaze into Seth's uncertain eyes. "Paddy's right. Things have changed. Now that my father is gone, I don't have to hide or worry about coming out." Mickey stared into Seth's hopeful eyes and wondered how he could ever have risked losing such a wonderful man.

The choice was easy.

"Seth. Baby. Sweet cheeks. I need *you*. I need you in my life. I need you standing beside me. I need your smiling face. And I need your warm heart. Without you, I'm lost. I promise to never keep you hidden in the shadows. I want you by my side. Always."

Seth's lip trembled as Mickey's words sunk in. "Are you sure?"

Mickey leaned forward and brought his lips to his own. "So? Will you be mine?" Mickey asked, assaulting Seth with his smoldering eyes.

"Just so we are clear. If I say yes, this also means you now belong to me. That means this dick belongs to me now. And it only comes out to play when I ask it to." Seth reached down between Mickey's legs and grabbed his quickly thickening cock, seeming to forget that they had an audience . . . or perhaps not caring.

"Fuck, yeah!" Mickey growled as he assaulted Seth's mouth like they were newlyweds on their honeymoon.

Patrick cleared his throat. "Are you guys done acting like horny teenagers?"

Seth chuckled and pulled away from Mickey while Mickey readjusted the tent in his joggers.

Leaning forward, Seth picked up the forgotten envelope and pulled out the pictures.

He flipped through the first few photos which showed someone dressed in black walking through the parking lot of the club, then passing the chef the box. Nothing seemed to stand out as unique or interesting.

When Seth got to the second to last photo, he stopped and stared at the person dressed in black. They were seated on their motorcycle, bent over, presumably about to drive off. The figure looked familiar.

Seth picked up his phone off the coffee table and began scrolling through the crime scene photos he kept on his phone . . . you know . . . just in case he ever needed to double-check something or wanted to verify some information.

God, if he ever had his phone confiscated . . . crime scene photos and Grindr dick pics . . . that's all they would ever see.

He stopped when he got to the photo of the alley where Jasper aka Beep was found dead. Mickey leaned over his shoulder and watched as Seth zoomed in on the photo.

He couldn't believe it. Standing at the end of the alleyway was a figure wearing the same black leather outfit and motorcycle helmet.

Oh, my god. They were there. Watching.

Seth could feel the excitement starting to build in his chest. He scrolled through a few more photos . . . hoping . . . then found it. Another photo with the same figure standing next to their motorcycle at the scene of Sven's murder.

Bingo. This had to be the killer.

"They were at all three of these scenes!" Seth gasped, flashing his phone at Mickey while he picked up the picture of the club once again.

Who is this guy? He was so close. He had to be.

Then Seth's eyes fell on something dark. Almost a smudge. There was something on their arm.

What is that?

Seth squinted and tried to make out what it was, but the image was too far away in the photo.

"You don't have this image on your phone or a laptop, do you?" Seth asked Patrick.

Mickey pulled out his phone from his back pocket and scrolled through the images. A moment later, Seth's phone buzzed with an incoming message. He clicked on the attachment and dragged his fingers across the image. His heart almost stopped in his chest.

"I don't fucking believe it." Seth's eyes were wide as he stared at the blown-up image of a rose surrounded by barbed wire.

"What? What is it?" Mickey asked, leaning forward to get a better look at the image.

"I've seen that tattoo before."

"What? On whom?" Mickey asked, tightening his grip on Seth's hips subconsciously.

Seth searched Mickey's hypnotic green eyes, wondering what he would do with the knowledge he was about to share. Would Mickey think rationally? Or would he fly off the handle in a murderous rage?

He needed to share this information, but he also needed to protect Mickey from himself.

"Look. I'll tell you who it is, but you have to promise me that you will remain calm and let us all work together to come up with a plan as to how to handle this situation."

Seth watched as Mickey's eye's darkened, and his lips thinned. This was the first time that Mickey had shown any anger toward Seth, and Seth was not a fan.

"Don't get all pissed at me. I'm looking out for you and don't want you getting hurt, you ass."

"Tell me who it fuckin' is. They killed my father and they almost killed you," Mickey growled, tightening his grip on Seth's arm.

Seth yanked his arm free with a force that surprised him. "Look. You are not going to intimidate me into giving you this information. I don't care how fucking tough you are. You're mine and I'm yours. That means we look out for each other. And that's what I'm trying to do. I'm going to tell you who it is, but I don't want you going all caveman on me and running off without a plan."

Mickey glared at Seth, clearly not used to having someone talk back to him. If they were going to be in a relationship, he better get used to it.

"Fine, no caveman behavior. How about angry Columbian?" Mickey countered sarcastically.

"No, I'd like to keep the body count to a minimum." Seth chuckled. He glanced at Patrick, who seemed surprised that Seth was able to control Mickey.

"So, who is it?"

"It's the teaching assistant I went to see last week about the formula Marc gave me. Ms. Sabrina Caine, I believe her name was."

"Caine? Don't think I know that name." Mickey turned to face Patrick, who was busy typing away on his phone.

The look of concentration on his face told them that he knew something.

"Shit. Just as I thought." Patrick leaned back onto the couch, glaring at Mickey.

"What? Who the fuck is she?"

Patrick turned his phone toward Mickey. "Do you recognize that guy?"

Mickey took the phone and stared at the picture. "Nah, who is he?"

"His name is Milton Caine. Son of Senator Charles Edward Caine," Patrick said as if that would answer all of Mickey's questions.

"So, why do I care that his father is a senator?"

"You might care because I used to be his dealer. He was one of our top customers. Bought coke off us almost daily. Then Beep informed me that his addiction was becoming bad. It was starting to affect his personal life."

Seth watched Mickey and Patrick exchange a look.

"What? Why do you care if it affects his personal life?"

"That's one of our rules. If we find out someone's addiction is starting to take over their lives, we cut them off. We stop selling to them. We sell drugs for recreation. We don't want it to ruin people's lives. So, what happened?" Mickey asked turning back to his second in command.

"Nothing. We cut him off and never spoke with him again."

Seth looked up from his phone. "It says here that Milton Caine died of an overdose six months ago. Perhaps that's why she's hunting down your men. She's out for revenge for killing her brother."

"But we didn't kill her brother," Patrick noted.

"Yeah, but perhaps she doesn't know that. She may just know that her brother bought his shit from you, so now she's coming after you guys thinking you are responsible for his death."

"Well, I've got a surprise for her." Mickey pulled out a gun and held it up in front of his face.

"Where the fuck did you pull that out of? Do I need to do a body cavity search every time we fuck?" Seth asked, alarmed at the sudden appearance of a gun.

"Don't be cute, sweet cheeks. I'm the only one doing any body cavity searches around here."

Seth's cheeks burned red. "Okay, before we go hunt this bitch down. I need to call my boss and get him up to speed."

"We don't need any help taking out a skinny bitch like her." Mickey was busy admiring the gun in his hand.

"That cut across your face and the destroyed condo says otherwise," Patrick noted.

If looks could kill, Patrick's brains would be splattered against the wall.

"My boss has a very particular set of skills that may help in this situation." Seth smirked.

"Fine. Call your boss." Mickey then turned to Patrick. "Get the boys together and have them meet us at the club tonight. Going to announce the changes in leadership and fill the crew in on what's been going on."

Patrick nodded, pulling out his cell phone and firing off texts.

"Oh, and I guess we need to start on funeral arrangements for my pops," Mickey's voice was soft and unsure.

"I'll get one of the wives to start on it," Mickey added, looking up from his phone momentarily.

Seth leaned back into Mickey's chest while he waited for Marc to answer his phone. They needed a plan of attack.

CHAPTER 25 - Mickey

It was just after midnight when Mickey pulled his Maserati into the parking spot next to Patrick's Porsche. These boys definitely loved their foreign cars.

Patrick was leaning against his car finishing a smoke while he waited for Mickey and Seth to exit their car.

Mickey had to give it to Patrick, while the guy was a total badass and scary as hell, the man always dressed with impeccable style. Tonight, he wore designer blue jeans, ripped just above the knees, and a thin black hoodie that gripped his muscular arms and chest. The zipper of the hoodie was pulled down just enough to show off part of his smooth bare chest.

Sometimes Mickey wondered if Patrick should give up a life of crime for the runways of Milan. The man looked fucking delicious.

"Waiting for your sugar daddy again, I see," Mickey

joked as he rounded the car and approached his best friend and now second in command.

"Someone has to keep me in the life I'm accustomed to. And when you're good at something, why give it away for free?" Paddy grabbed his bulge and gave it a squeeze.

"You two have some serious issues." Seth joined the two while Patrick finished his smoke.

"Nah, we just know each other too well." Patrick smirked as he tossed his smoke across the parking lot. "Let's go set these boys straight."

Patrick led the way, followed by Mickey with Seth trailing behind. They entered through the back of The Lady's Touch strip club and followed Patrick down the cold metal steps into the basement.

When not being used as Patrick's torture chamber, the basement doubled as a meeting room. A place where important announcements were made and sensitive jobs were discussed. There were no recording devices and no interruptions from unwanted guests.

The room went silent when Mickey and Patrick reached the bottom of the stairs. All the team leaders of the crew were in attendance, which included Ian, Brody, Dominic, Shawn, Rian, and a few others who had grown up with Clive O'Brien and were nearing retirement. They were the men Mickey relied on to oversee various aspects of their operation. Each team leader managed their own teams that all rolled up into Mickey.

He was relying on these guys to ensure that word

spread of his father's passing and the new organizational structure of their crew. The organization was much too big for one man to manage.

Brody eyed Seth as he trailed in behind Mickey and Patrick. Seth met his gaze and quickly looked away. Sensing his discomfort, Mickey grabbed Seth by the hand and walked with him toward the group of confused-looking men.

The crew stood huddled in the center of the room, some enjoying a beer as they waited for their boss to arrive.

Mickey released Seth's hand and stepped up onto a small crate to give himself a bit of a height over everyone else. Patrick took his place to the right side of Mickey and turned to face the crew with his arms firmly crossed against his chest.

Seth found a spot to the left of where Mickey stood, trying to remain out of the crew's line of sight.

"Thanks for coming, gents. I know it's late and everyone is busy with their families, but I have some important things to discuss that couldn't wait until the morning."

"Sorry to hear about your pops! He was a good man!" Ian shouted from where he stood. He raised his beer in the air, saluting Mickey and his dead father.

The rest of the group followed suit.

"Thanks, buddy. Pops was a good man, and he will be missed. That's part of the reason why I called this meeting.

As you know, head of this crew now falls to me. I'll be assumin' control of all of Pop's operations, dealin's, and assets.

"Paddy, get the word out to all our business associates and let them know that they do business with me now. Brody, get the word out to the street crew and teams, letting them know about the change in management. Dom, you and I are going to meet next week to go over finances and the books. I want to know where every last dollar is and how it's being spent.

"Patrick will continue to be my number two. So, you bring him any problems or issues. This is a family; we don't cover shit up. I want to know everything that goes on in this crew. If we have a problem, we work together to fix it. Am I clear?"

"Yeah, boss," Rian answered as the group nodded their heads.

Good. So far everything was going smoothly. Now for the hard stuff.

"This brings me to the second issue I wanted to discuss with you tonight. Over the past few months, we have lost Bernard, Sven, Beep, and now my father. Their deaths were no accident." Mickey paused, letting this news sink in.

The group of men looked around at one another, some whispering among themselves, some shaking their heads in disbelief.

"What do you mean, Mick?" one of the older members asked.

"It appears that they were being hunted and killed by a woman who thinks we killed her brother." Mickey watched their reactions carefully. He wanted to see if he needed to worry about any of his guys overreacting or taking matters into their own hands. "We know who this bitch is, and we have a plan to take her down."

A few of the guys stepped forward, eyes blazing at the thought that the deaths of their brothers had not been accidents as first thought.

"What do you need us to do?" Dominic asked.

Even though Dominic was their "finance" guy, he never shied away from a fight and always did what he could to show the guys that even though he was Italian, he was still one of their Irish brothers.

He was sweet, loyal, and smart as fuck . . . but when you crossed him, watch out. The guy was vicious. It was that Sicilian temper that scared the shit out of people. Had he been born across the river, the New York Italians would have scooped him up in an instant. Instead, he had been born in Jersey—the rough part of Jersey. So, that meant, he belonged with the Irish.

Mickey spent the next twenty minutes laying out the plan he and Seth's friend, Marc, had developed. He had to admit, Marc was a fucking genius when it came to strategizing and accounting for all scenarios and contingencies.

Mickey, on the other hand, was the resources guy. He had the crew and the muscle needed to execute this masterful plan.

The guys nodded and followed along as he laid out their plan and everyone's assignments. A few got confused when he tried to explain setting up diversions and blocking off some of the access points, so he tried to keep things simple. Park truck here, post sign there. Ignore all questions. Simple.

When he was done explaining the plan, he glanced at Seth, who was staring up at him with admiration. He felt like a Gladiator about to lead his men into battle. Mickey couldn't help the feeling of pride in having Seth by his side. He didn't want to keep such a wonderful man a secret.

"Also, I wanted to introduce you to Seth"—Mickey gestured his hand toward a startled Seth—"my boyfriend." He gave Seth a loving smile, then turned back to face his crew.

The guys all stood silent, eyes wide, mouths gaping. Not one of them moved or said a thing.

Mickey stepped off the crate and took a step forward. "Does anyone have an issue with this?" He dared anyone to speak up.

He eyed the room full of men, many of whom he had grown up with and even a few who had shared women with him at orgies and sex parties.

His eyes fell on Brody, who refused to look up from his shoes.

"You got something you want to say, Brody?"

"Nah, man. No—nothin' from me."

"Just so we're clear here. The old ways died with my father. I won't stand for any backward homophobic bullshit. This here is a family! We will treat each other with love and respect.

"If you have a problem with someone, you come to me. I have always looked out for this family, and I will continue to look out for this family," Mickey's voice was firm and commanding as he addressed the men before him. This was his crew. He was the boss. "And, if this is something you can't live with, there is the door. But just know, that if you leave, you will be leaving this family as well. Any questions?"

All guys, including Brody, stood firmly in their spots. The entire crew shook their heads. Brody finally lifted his gaze to meet Mickey's. He looked like a child who had just been scolded by his father but now wanted a hug. It was funny how kids reacted like that.

"I got somethin' to say," a voice called from the back of the crowd.

Patrick took a protective step forward as Mickey raised his arm, signaling him to stop.

From the back of the crowd, Joe Murphy, his father's old friend stepped forward.

Mickey's eyes locked with Joe's. This was a man he had grown up with, a man he respected. A man who had even witnessed his father's brutal attack on his childhood friend's gay father.

"Please, speak." Mickey gestured to the man.

"I'll be honest, it pains me to watch you stand here tonight explaining to us why you have the right to love who you love.

"I have known you since you were a wee lad and I've watched ya grow into the strong man you are today. We don't follow you because you are tough or because we're afraid of you. We follow you because we respect you. You're the type of man who looks out for his crew, who organizes football camps for kids, and helps elderly people mow their lawns. And I guess it hurts me to see that you don't see yourself the way we see you.

"You're not a monster. And we certainly don't give a shit who you stick your dick into."

The crowd laughed.

"All's we care about is you, Mickey."

Mickey swallowed the lump in his throat. He had spent his whole life seeing himself as a monster, or a demon. He secretly hoped that by doing good deeds, he might somehow atone for the sins he had committed.

Hearing Joe's words broke through the darkness and lifted all the worry and guilt he was feeling. He never knew that the crew felt this way about him.

Mickey walked up to his father's oldest friend and wrapped his arms around him. "Thank you, Joe," Mickey whispered.

"I meant every word, captain."

Mickey chuckled. He pulled away and slapped Joe on the back, then turned back to the crew. "Okay, everyone, go home to your families and I'll see you all tomorrow."

Several of the guys approached Mickey to give him their condolences and then gave Seth a pat on the back, welcoming him to the "family."

Mickey watched as Brody dragged his feet toward Seth.

"Everything okay here?" Mickey asked, placing his arm around Seth. He knew Brody would never do anything to harm Seth in front of him, but he wanted Seth to feel safe and secure. Seth had only had the one bad encounter with Brody so far.

Brody rubbed the back of his neck as he stared down at his shoes. He looked scared and nervous. It was strange seeing him this way, considering the man liked to box as a hobby.

"Look, I just wanted to apologize for the way I acted back in the bar, that other time." Brody glanced up at Seth. "I was bein' a dick and shouldn't have said that shit to ya."

Patrick joined the group and placed his hand around the back of Brody's neck, making him flinch.

"Everything good here?" Patrick glanced at Brody but was speaking to Mickey.

"Yeah, man. I was just apologizin' to Mickey's new guy, hoping to make things right," Brody responded, glancing bashfully at Seth.

Seth stuck out his hand to Brody. "It's all good. I appreciate you saying that."

Brody took his hand and gave it a firm shake. "Thanks, brother, I appreciate it. If it helps, Paddy fucked up my face that night pretty good." Brody gave Patrick a half-smile.

The group laughed.

"Tried to make you better lookin', but sadly, failed." Patrick patted Brody on the back as he turned to go speak with an older, balding gentleman.

CHAPTER 26- Seth

"Here. Now we are all patched in," Marc said, as he passed the laptop to Seth.

Seth adjusted the laptop in his lap and placed the earpiece into his right ear. His adrenaline was pumping. Part of him was excited to finally take out the bitch who almost killed him, but part of him was also terrified that something would go wrong.

Breathe, Seth kept telling himself over and over. Marc had designed the plan, and Mickey had laid out the players. They were golden. He had to have faith that each player knew their parts, including himself.

"You nervous?" Marc asked.

"Kind of. Just scared something might go wrong."

"That's why you have Alex and me here to help you. You know I've looked at every possible scenario and have three backup plans in place, just in case. One of them even involved blowing up that bitch's house while she sleeps."

Seth chuckled. Marc had suggested that as plan number three, but Alex shot it down as it would draw too much attention. He hoped Marc had listened to him.

"Thanks, man. You and Alex have been great."

Marc took a sip of his black coffee and then adjusted some buttons on his coms. "So, tell me about this *drug lord* you're madly in love with? Does he treat you right?"

Seth gave Marc an annoyed look. "Yes, for your information, he is sweet and kind and has taken care of me on more than one occasion."

"More than one?"

"There was an incident involving pink drinks, projectile vomiting, and a bathtub." Seth watched as Marc burst into a fit of laughter.

"Enough said. As long as you're happy, Seth. You know Alex and I think of you as our little brother, so if this Casanova does anything to hurt you or break your heart, I will disappear him. Starting with his two Cayman Island accounts, then moving on to the house he has in Mykonos, before ending with the storage unit in Boston. Bottom line, they will find his body in a cabin somewhere along with a suicide note."

"Wow, you really did your homework on this one." Seth laughed, wondering how much of what Marc said was true and how much was just a joke. Marc wasn't known for his humor.

"I get it. Treat Seth like the king that he is, or you will destroy my life," Mickey's voice came through on the coms.

Seth's mouth dropped open. He had no idea Marc had turned on the coms and that Mickey was listening in on their private conversation.

"Glad we have an understanding. Seth is a good man and part of my family, and I protect my family." Marc winked at Seth, who was staring at him speechless.

"I couldn't agree with you more. Seth is mine now, and I protect what is mine. So, I guess, Seth is now the safest man in Jersey." Mickey chuckled.

"What about me? I'm feeling a little left out over here. Why do we need to watch from the damn roof anyway?" Alex's annoyed voice came in over the coms.

"How many people are on this fucking call?" Seth seethed. Suddenly this was becoming the party line from hell.

"I'm always in Marc's head. Think of me as Jiminy Cricket. I'm the voice of reason and his conscience, if you will," Alex chirped back.

"It's just the four of us. Alex is always on coms with me cuz I have issues with being separated from him."

"You might want to unpack that one on here. Sounds like something we should talk about," Mickey chimed in sarcastically.

"I don't share my feelings with guys I don't know," Marc commented.

"You have feelings?" Seth joked.

"Okay. How about we get back to the purple dust lady . . . you know, the one who tried to kill you with your dreams?"

There was something sarcastic about the way Marc described the murder weapon. If Freddy could murder people in their sleep, why couldn't a chemist?

"You're right. Everyone in position?" Seth pulled up the surveillance cameras in Ms. Caine's office and watched the live feed.

"Roger," multiple voices responded, signaling that they were all ready.

Seth watched as Ms. Caine sat down behind her desk and switched on her laptop. She failed to notice the tiny cameras hidden throughout her office and paid no notice when her laptop camera activated.

Seth and Marc both watched as the woman opened a new web browser and began logging into her university web account.

It was time for the games to begin.

Seth typed in a series of codes on his laptop and watched as Caine's computer screen went black. Judging by the confused look on her face, they had her attention.

With the stroke of a button, the woman's screen

reactivated, displaying a blurred-out image of Seth's face.

Caine glanced around her office, confused and unsettled.

"I finally get the significance of the rose and barbwire tattoo. Even something so beautiful can have deadly consequences. Suiting, I guess," Seth greeted.

"Who are you? What do you want?" Caine demanded.

"This little game of yours is over. You have two options. You can either pick up the phone, call the police, and explain to them how you created a lethal drug that you then used to murder four innocent men . . . " Seth waited and watched the woman on the screen smirk at him.

"Not going to happen, jackass," Caine's shrill voice responded.

"Or you can choose option number two."

"And what's that?"

"My friends and I hunt *you* down and end *your* life."

Marc smiled at the image on the screen: The woman had picked up a hair tie and was tying her hair up in a tight ponytail. Next, she took off her reading glasses and placed them down on the table next to the laptop.

"She's choosing option two," Marc whispered.

"What? How do you know that?" Seth asked, watching the image on the screen for any telltale signs.

"She's preparing to run—tying up the hair, removing

the glasses, next you'll see her pull out a weapon."

Sure enough, she reached into her bag and pulled out a gun.

Seth's mouth dropped open. "How did you . . . ?"

Marc just shrugged his shoulder.

Seth felt anger flare within him. Even after all of this, this bitch still wanted to fight. Seth pressed a button on his laptop.

"It looks like you're choosing option number two . . . Your death. See you in hell, bitch." Seth switched off Caine's computer screen and then turned off all the lights in her office.

They listened to her squeal in surprise. Next, Seth took control of the speaker system in her office and blasted NSYNC's *Bye Bye Bye*.

Seth heard Mickey and Alex chuckle over the coms.

"You're savage," Alex said.

"Guys, get ready. She's about to run, and she's carrying a gun," Seth warned, ignoring Alex's comment.

They watched as Caine grabbed her purse and ran out of her office. Five minutes later, they spotted her running through the parking lot and hopping on her motorcycle before speeding off.

"Dom, Professor Peabody is headed your way."

"Gotcha. Detour is in place. By the way, we should

totally trade playlists," Dom said.

More laughter from Mickey and Alex.

"Hey, there is nothing wrong with NSYNC. Love me some boyband shit," Seth argued.

"I'll buy you the complete collection as well as the Irish bootlegs that are hard to come by. And by the way, Dom was being serious. He's a big Backstreet Boys fan. You should see him on a dancefloor," Mickey responded.

"It always gets the ladies where they need to be . . . on my face," Dom added.

"And the boys," Mickey quipped.

This time, Seth and Alex were laughing. Dom was silent.

"This is why I prefer to work alone," Marc grumbled.

"Yeah, I kind of get Unabomber feels from you, my friend," Mickey couldn't help adding.

"How about I take you up to my cabin sometime and we can do a bit of bonding?" Marc calmly replied, his tone unsettling even for Seth.

"Something tells me that my answer should be a hard no and I should get my ass back to work," Mickey answered.

"That would be wise, babe," Seth added, following the tracker they placed on Caine's motorcycle through his laptop. "Dom, she should be approaching you in a minute."

"I see her. She's turning down Lexington as we wanted. Ian, she's headed your way," Dom said.

Marc and Seth made their way to the warehouse by the docks, where the detours were leading Caine.

Mickey's crew had arranged road closures and blockades strategically throughout the city, leaving only one path for Caine to follow.

CHAPTER 27- Mickey

The roar of the approaching motorcycle could be heard from two streets away. She was almost here. It was time to meet this woman face to face and end this right here and now.

Mickey stood in front of the warehouse as he watched the black motorcycle turn onto his property and speed toward him. Apparently, she was done playing around as well.

Caine braked hard, causing the backend of the bike to lift up in the air and spin into a 180-degree turn. She spun expertly and then bounced gracefully when the bike touched the ground.

She killed the engine and stepped off the bike. Mickey watched as the woman removed her helmet and flipped her ponytail over her shoulder. The woman knew how to make an entrance.

Mickey walked down the ratty steps of the warehouse and took a few steps toward her.

"Remember, don't get too close. We don't want her dousing you with another hit of her purple magic," Seth said through the tiny piece in his ear.

It was a little frustrating hearing the voice of his sweet cheeks but not being able to see him. It had only been a few hours, but he already missed the feel of Seth's perfect ass cheeks in the palm of his hands.

Focus, Mickey . . .

"That's far enough," Mickey commanded from where he stood at the bottom of the steps.

"Oh, c'mon now, is that any way to speak to a guest?" Caine gave an evil grin as she stopped her advance.

"You've already killed four members of my crew, including my father. Don't mind me if I keep my distance."

"So that means your twerp of a boyfriend survived? I take it that was him on the screen this morning?"

Mickey nodded.

"Too bad. I was hoping you were the last one on my hit list, but it sounds like I have to pay your little friend a visit after this."

Mickey's eyes slowly moved up to the third floor of the adjacent building. Something flickered, catching Mickey's eye. It was the reflection from the scope attached to Patrick's rifle. They couldn't be too careful.

Now it was time for some answers.

"Why are you doing this?"

Caine chuckled. "Isn't it obvious? You killed my fucking brother," the coldness in her voice spoke volumes. This was personal for her. She was avenging the death of her brother.

"I'm sorry to hear that your brother died. But we didn't kill him."

Caine took two steps forward and stopped. "You guys gave him the fucking coke that killed him, you piece of shit."

Mickey shook his head. "No, that wasn't us. Yes, we used to sell to your brother, but a few months before his death we realized his drug use was getting out of control, so we cut him off. We wouldn't sell to him anymore."

Caine stared at him with daggers in her eyes. "You're lying. All you dirtbags are the same. You don't care who you hurt, or how many lives you destroy. All's you care about is filling your pockets with dirty money."

"I don't give a shit if you believe me or not. You killed three of my friends, my father, then you tried to kill the man I love. Now you're going to suffer, bitch." Mickey's fists tightened as he tried to maintain control of his anger, which was something he was never very good at.

He needed to remain focused.

Caine snickered at him. "Like to see you try, shit for brains. Why don't you come a little closer and we can have a little chat, face to face."

"As tempting as that is, I prefer to keep my distance until I know your Purple Dust has been neutralized."

"And how do you propose to do that?"

"I may not have gone to college or even finished high school, but if I'm not mistaken, if you want to neutralize a base you add water. Well, you're the chemistry doctor person, am I right?" Mickey took a step forward as he shrugged his shoulders.

"Well, not exactly . . . but you're on the right line of thinking. Perhaps you're not as stupid as you look."

"I find that people are always underestimating me. I think it's the good looks and big muscles. Seth, baby, are you ready?"

"Oh, yeah."

Caine jumped at the sound of Seth's voice right next to her.

Seth gave her an evil grin as he opened the valve to a high-pressed fire hose that Mickey kept around for emergencies.

Caine screamed as Seth doused her body from head to toe, making sure to drench her purse, jacket, and even her hair. He wanted to make sure that any traces of Purple Dust were soaked, rendering the toxin useless against them.

"Not so tough now, ninja bitch." Seth increased the pressure on the hose, throwing her off balance and knocking her to her knees.

Once he was satisfied that she had been thoroughly watered, he turned off the hose and gave Marc the thumbs up.

They all watched as the woman began to sob. Surprisingly, they felt no shame or pity for her. There was no urge to apologize or rush to comfort her. They simply watched on with suspicion.

"Are you done yet?" Mickey asked. "I'll give you one last chance to choose option one. If you call the police and confess to your crimes, we will let you live. We have both lost people unnecessarily."

"Go fuck yourself!" Caine screamed as she reached inside her purse.

The sound of a gunshot rang through the air.

Mickey lunged toward Seth instinctively to protect him.

Instead, he found Seth pointing a revolver at Caine. Her vacant eyes stared upward, as a trickle of blood spilled from the bullet hole smoking in her forehead. The gun she held slid from her hand and made a clanking sound as it hit the concrete below.

The world fell silent as Mickey rushed to where Seth stood in shock.

"She was going to shoot you?" Seth mumbled, eyes never leaving Caine's lifeless body.

"I know. And you saved my life." Mickey grabbed Seth's face in both of his hands and stared into his once gentle eyes. "You did what you had to do. Otherwise, I would be dead."

Seth blinked a few times, seeming to clear the fog from his mind. "Yes, I had no choice."

Mickey pulled him close and held him tightly in his arms. Patrick, Marc, and the others came running out from their tactical positions.

"Is he okay?" Alex asked, brushing a concerned hand through Seth's brown locks.

"He will be. Your first kill is always a lot to take in." Mickey glanced at Marc, who gave a knowing look.

CHAPTER 28 – Seth

He looked so peaceful laying there under the gentle kiss of the morning sun. It had been two weeks since Seth put a bullet in Ms. Caine's brain, and he was still having trouble sleeping through the night.

Mickey had been amazing. He was attentive, patient, and always there when Seth felt like he was about to have a freakout. His calming words and ability to listen to Seth vent, even when his words did not make sense, added to the numerous qualities Seth was falling in love with. And to think, this all started with a drink at a bar.

Seth placed his head against Mickey's bare chest and listened to his heartbeat as he slept. God—he loved this man. He gently placed his hand on Mickey's chest and leaned into the warmth of his body. This was his favorite part—lying in bed cuddling up against his man.

Seth smiled as he felt Mickey's rough paw land on his

shoulder. A second later, Mickey sucked in a deep breath as he yawned.

The beast was waking up.

Mickey pulled Seth's body tight against his own. His muscles flexed and bulged as Seth basked in the feeling of being protected in the loving arms of his man.

It was time for breakfast.

Seth kissed Mickey's chest and then made his way down his man's chiseled body. He loved the V-thingy that surrounded Mickey's pelvis.

From above his head, he listened to his man groan as he realized what was happening. Seth continued on his journey down under the sheets until he came to Mickey's rock-solid morning wood.

Seth licked his lips, then swallowed his man's shaft in one gulp. He loved listening to Mickey moan. Knowing he was the cause of such pleasure.

Slowly, he sucked his cock nice and deep, being sure to pay special attention to Mickey's balls. As it turned out, Mickey loved having his balls played with while Seth was giving him head.

Using his other hand to grip his shaft, Seth increased his speed, sucking fast and deep, taking in every inch until he felt Mickey's balls tighten, then tasted the sweetness of Mickey's release as he unloaded down his throat.

Seth swallowed every last drop of his man's seed. He loved servicing this hot slab of beef each morning, knowing that each night it was his man who would be servicing him. Pounding every last inch of that thick dick into his tight hole. Fuck—he loved it.

A strong hand reached under the sheets and pulled Seth back against his chest.

"Mornin', sweet cheeks." Mickey leaned in and gave Seth a loving kiss.

"Morning, my sexy stud." Seth grinned like a kid on Christmas morning.

"So, what do you have planned for today?"

"I'm going to have coffee this morning with my gran. I haven't seen her much since the fight with my parents."

Mickey caressed Seth's back while his head rested on Mickey's chest.

"Are you going to finally tell me what really happened between you and your folks?" Mickey asked in a cautious tone.

Seth's body stiffened. It wasn't that he didn't want to tell Mickey what happened, it was that he felt embarrassed by his parents' betrayal. Parents were supposed to be there for their children, but in Seth's case, they'd turned their back on him.

Feeling the tension in Seth's body, Mickey kissed the top of Seth's head. "Don't worry. If you're not ready to share that with me, I understand."

Sensing the disappointment in Mickey's voice, Seth sat

up in bed to get a better view of his face. "Babe, please don't ever think I don't feel comfortable telling you things or that I don't trust you. The reason I'm hesitant to tell you is that I'm embarrassed." Seth sat cross-legged in bed, staring at his hands in his lap.

Mickey sat up in bed, giving Seth his full attention. "Hey, you have nothing to ever feel embarrassed about with me. I love you for who you are, the good, the bad, *and* the crazy." Mickey rubbed Seth's leg hoping.

How had he gotten so lucky to have met such a wonderful guy? Seth decided to share his greatest embarrassment with the man he loved. He took a deep breath, then began, "My father is a big-time corporate lawyer in Chicago. He and Eric, his best friend from college, opened a large firm together when I was just a kid. Two years ago, Eric hired me to work as one of his interns so I could get some work experience and earn a bit of extra cash. I think my dad secretly hoped I would change my mind and want to go into corporate law.

"Anyway, over time, Eric began flirting with me and making inappropriate sexual comments. He was married with three kids, and my dad's best friend.

"One weekend, I was working late at the office with Eric when he suggested we go back to his place and have some fun since his wife and kids were away for the weekend. I told him I wasn't interested, but he kept insisting to the point I was worried he might try and rape me. I ended up finding an opportunity to leave and went home to tell my parents.

"They, of course, didn't believe me. They thought I was making the story up as a way to get out of working with my father. And why would a happily married, straight man be hitting on his young gay intern?

"I felt so angry that my parents refused to believe me. They chose to believe the word of a cheating sleaze bag over their son, so I left. I felt so betrayed by my parents. They were the ones who were supposed to be on my side. To protect me. But in their eyes, I was nothing but a liar. That's why I'm embarrassed to tell people the real reason I don't speak with my parents. Parents are supposed to protect their kids, not throw them to the wolves."

Mickey placed his fingers underneath Seth's chin and lifted his head so they were staring at one another. "I believe you. I'm so sorry that you have shit parents. But I am here now. I'm your family. I will always believe you and protect you. I promise you that."

A tear slid down Seth's face as he lunged into Mickey's open arms.

This was exactly what he needed. Someone who believed him, loved him, and would always protect him. His heart belonged to Mickey.

Seth leaned into Mickey's warm embrace and basked in the safety and security of his arms. They lay there holding each other as they watched the sunrise over downtown Jersey.

This was love.

Epilogue- Mickey

Music vibrated through the walls as Mickey pulled open the door that connected The Lady's Touch with The Stud's Embrace, the hottest new gay strip club in Jersey.

It had been nine months since Ms. Caine's reign of terror ended with a bullet to the brain and a confused police force. While the police had their suspicions as to what happened that sunny morning, they had a little difficulty proving anything, especially when witnesses' stories kept changing and evidence kept being misplaced.

Mickey had successfully taken over his father's enterprise with minimal pushback from competing gangs. Most had worked with Mickey in the past, so they already knew and respected him, which made for an easy transition of power.

No one seemed to care or even mention the fact that Mickey was in a committed relationship with a man. Although Seth suspected that some may just be too terrified of Mickey and Patrick to dare say anything. Either way, it made life easier when they didn't have to hide their relationship.

As luck would have it, the owner of the bar next to The Lady's Touch decided to suddenly retire and move to warmer climates for medical reasons. Seth had a suspicion that Patrick may have been part of that "medical reason."

A few days before, Seth had casually mentioned how it would be cool to open a gay strip club right next to Mickey's straight one. A few days later, the owner was selling. Happy coincidence?

Seth explained that if Mickey installed a door between the two properties, the club could maximize profits by offering "closeted" men an alternative entrance to the gay club—through the straight club. Men could enter through the doors of the straight strip club, then use the more discreet entrance inside the club to enter the adjoining gay strip club. Mickey and Dominic loved the idea.

The idea was for Mickey to continue to run The Lady's Touch while Seth would manage The Stud's Embrace next door. This gave Seth a steady income, and it allowed them to work together on nights when Mickey was at the Club.

"No, no. No. Stop the music!" Seth shouted at the man sitting in the DJ booth.

Mickey watched as Seth got up from his table and walked to where five men in various stages of undress were standing on stage.

"When you're dancing on stage, you are creating art! You are creating a fantasy! I want to see emotion and passion! You need to look into every guy's eye and let him know you are offering him a lifetime of romance, protection, and the hottest sex he has ever had! You are not 'strippers,' you are 'performers!'

Seth stared at the men on stage. While Mickey's club was your traditional tits-and-ass-in-your-face strip club, Seth wanted to offer a much classier experience. He wanted to create a fantasy world, where queer men could come and experience their every desire. It wasn't just sex he was selling; it was an experience.

"Looking good, babe," Mickey called from the shadows.

Seth's face lit up when Mickey emerged from the darkness.

"How is it that you get hotter every time I see you? Got time to take me upstairs and fuck my brains out?" Seth smiled at him with heated eyes.

"I will take you up on that later, but first, I have something special for you. Guys, how about you wrap it up for the day? We'll see you tonight for your shift." Mickey took Seth's hand and led him to a booth near the bar. He helped his love into the seat and slid in next to him. "Here, hope you like." Mickey slid Seth a brown file folder and placed his arm around Seth's shoulders.

"What's this?" Seth opened the file and flipped through photos of his father's business partner, Eric, and Nicky, one of their gay dancers.

With each photo, the images got raunchier and raunchier, finally culminating with an image of Nicky blowing Eric.

"Oh my god," Seth's voice was low as he stared at the final photo.

"Nicky offered to help me nail that bastard for what he did to you. Right now, these photos are being couriered to Eric's wife and your parents."

Mickey's phone beeped with an incoming text message.

"Looks like the package was just delivered to his wife." Mickey showed Seth his phone, confirming that the package had been accepted by a Mrs. Bromson.

His phone dinged again.

"And now it looks like your parents just received theirs. I'm sorry I didn't ask for your permission before I went ahead and did this, but the thought of this asshole hurting you and destroying your relationship with your folks is something I cannot live with. I told you I would protect you always, so this is me protecting you."

Mickey held his breath while he waited for Seth's reaction. He worried that perhaps he had gone too far, but he needed to get justice for the man he loved. And what better way than to destroy the bastard's life?

Seth was staring at the photos, not moving.

"Seth? I'm sorry if I . . . " Mickey's words were cut off when Seth raised his head and wiped a tear from his cheek.

"Thank you," Seth's voice was soft and gentle. "It

means so much knowing that you will always defend me and stand up for me. Every time I think I can't love you anymore, you do something like this." Seth leaned forward and attacked his lips.

Seth's kiss was passionate and deep. Mickey wrapped his arms around his man and pulled him tight against his chest.

"I'm always here for you, sweet cheeks. Will love you till the end."

Seth's phone began to ring.

He fished it out of his pocket and dropped it on the table when he saw the word on the screen. "Shit, it's my mom. What do I do?"

"It's up to you. You have an opportunity to listen to what she has to say, and then you can decide how you want to proceed. You don't have to forgive your parents just yet, but you can hear them out. Whatever you decide to do, I will support you, babe." Mickey squeezed Seth's thigh, falling in love with the man all over again.

With the swipe of his finger, Seth brought the phone to his ear and listened to his mother's tearful voice.

Mickey walked to the bar and poured them both a glass of whiskey. Seth normally drank fancy cocktails, but the regular bartender would not be in for another few hours, and fuck if Mickey knew how to make one.

He brought the drinks back to the booth, sliding one to Seth as he listened to him taking the first steps toward mending the bridge with his parents.

While it may take a while for Seth to completely forgive his parents for their betrayal, Mickey would be there supporting him every step of the way.

Seth was Mickey's as much as Mickey was Seth's. For the first time in his life, Mickey was excited to see what the future would bring. A future with Seth by his side.

ABOUT THE AUTHOR

Matthew Dante is a Canadian Indie author who writes thriller, romance, and fantasy stories. He graduated with a Major in Criminology and has been working in the financial crimes industry for over 20 years. He is an avid reader, world traveler, lover of all things Marvel and DC, and a romantic at heart.

As an Indie author, your reviews are very important. They help others take a chance on a new author and discover books that they might not have noticed in the past. So, if you enjoyed this book, please consider taking a few moments to leave a review.

To stay up to date on all the latest news, follow Matthew Dante on Instagram, Facebook, Goodreads, and Bookbub.

Thanks again for taking the time to read this book. Your love and support mean the world to me.

ACKNOWLEDGEMENT

Thank you to my wonderful and supportive family. Without you, I would not have the courage and strength to chase after my dreams. You have always been that voice of encouragement cheering me on.

Thank you to Stefka, Maryann, Michael, Garry, and the rest of my beta and ARC readers, who have read through the various versions of this book and provided valuable notes, suggestions, and feedback.

To Anna, your cover design and amazing promos have helped to bring the vision of my story to life. Your talent is truly extraordinary.

Lastly, I wanted to thank you, the reader. It is because of you that Seth has been given his own book. Many people reached out demanding that the sweet and feisty twink be given his own book. So, here it is. I hope you enjoyed his story and continue to enjoy the next book in this series. I'm thinking it will involve a certain hot-tempered, boyband-loving Italian money launderer . . .

OTHER BOOKS BY MATTHEW DANTE

Suspense/Thriller Books

FRACTURED SERIES

Fractured Love (Book 1)

Fractured Mind (Book 2)

Fractured Soul (Book 3)

A ROUGE EDGES SERIES

Laying Claim (Book 1)

Romance Books

Love to Hate You

The Devil Wears Pink (Cruising: An MM Anthology)

Fantasy Books

THE DARK SORCERER SERIES

The Prophecy (Book 1)

Rise of the Dark Sorcerer (Book 2)

THE DARK BLOOD SERIES

Dark Blood (Book 1)

LAYING CLAIM